4/4/89

LIONS · TEEN TRACKS

Breaking Up

Monday March 16th

'I'm supposed to have scored a girlfriend today. This girl, Cathy Roussos, reckons she's been rapt in me since the beginning of the year. Today in the canteen, her friend, Rosie, came up to Billy and me and asked Billy if Cathy and me were going together.

Billy sort of started acting like my manager and said to Rosie, "Maybe. Does she want to go with Mark?"

And Rosie said, "Maybe. Does Mark want to go with her?"

Billy said, "Maybe." When she walked away, Billy turned around with a big smile on his mug and bashed me on the arm. "You're in. You've scored," he said. So I'm sort of going with Cathy . . .'

This is an extract from fifteen-year-old Mark Wheeler's diary, in which he writes about school, friends, girls and home in the year in which his family breaks up.

Also available in Lions Teen Tracks

Frank Willmott

Breaking Up

LIONS · TEEN TRACKS

First published in Great Britain 1983
by William Collins Sons & Co. Ltd
First published in Lions Teen Tracks 1983
Fifth impression August 1988

Lions Teen Tracks is an imprint of
the Children's Division, part of
the Collins Publishing Group,
8 Grafton Street, London W1X 3LA

Printed and bound in Great Britain by
William Collins Sons & Co. Ltd, Glasgow

To my friend Billy. What ever became of you?
Someone else lives in your flat.

FOREWORD

My name is Mark Wheeler, I'm sixteen now, and I live in Melbourne, Australia. No kidding, it took me just three months to write this book, and I'm still attending school. One thing I've got to admit; it wasn't so hard writing it. For a start I've got to thank Paul Kelly, my English teacher last year, because he really started the book by making me write and keep up a diary. As you'll find out, the book is really just the diary entries put together.

After a while I got the hang of keeping a diary and began to enjoy it. Paul Kelly used to check it, but he never marked it or anything like that. Anyway I found it better to write things down in my diary instead of holding them inside my head and letting them get diseased – you know what I mean? Especially when things got pretty tough last year. I also wrote the book for other kids who go through the same problems at home as we did.

Mark Wheeler
August 1982.

Monday March 2nd 1981

Today in English, we talked all about how to keep a diary, and the sorts of things to write in it. Paul Kelly, our teacher, says we have to have a special book for it, and he would be rapt if some people could keep it up for the whole year. He said to try and write about the most important thing that happens during the day, and if nothing happens, then just talk about things that have happened in the past that are interesting memories, or about the things you want to get off your chest. He reckons it's better to get down quickly what's going on in your brain and how you feel about it, instead of worrying about writing perfectly.

I'm going to start and talk about my little brother Andy. He's three years younger than me. One of the first things I remember about him was when he was five, and went over the front handle-bars of his trike. He smashed his two front teeth through the flesh above his lip which made him look like a rhinoceros. The doctor said to leave them sticking out and they'd fall off by themselves. Some kids wouldn't go near him. He used to stare in the mirror pulling all these animal faces, waiting for the second tooth to fall off.

I don't remember him as a baby, just this chubby little kid walking around in circles in our old backyard, circles that got smaller and smaller until he wrapped himself around the clothes-line and fell to the ground dead. He wheezes a lot because he's had asthma since a kid, and Jackie, that's my mum, watches over him like a hawk. But he's never acted like an invalid. He's always involved in some weird adventure of his own, always hurting himself –

9

but never crying; just talking or swearing to himself. He loves to prop his bedclothes up with sticks and talk in his little indoor tent; and I've got to share a room with that sort of childish behaviour.

We never really muck around together any more. Once he had to go everywhere I did, but now he just wants to do weird things by himself. And if we have a game of footy or cricket or something, he won't take it seriously and is always mucking around or getting bored or walking off in the middle of it. I only ever tried to tell him about girls once.

Tuesday March 3rd

The school I go to is crazy. The kids are crazy. It's an old red brick building found amongst factories with new parts joined on, like the library and Creative Arts block, and port- ables are scattered around the small yard. It's supposed to be one of those experimental schools, and the students are the guinea-pigs. It is divided up into four smaller mini-schools which all have their own way of running things. The kids reckon that the school's a pushover; so do their parents; and kids who go to other schools are always telling you the same.

"They just have old ideas on how you learn," says Alec, my dad. "They think continual silence and writing means learning. That's only baby-sitting."

He runs one of the mini-schools. That's right, my dad is a teacher, and my mum was once also. His Area is the worst. If you go down there you will find kids running around and laughing and wrestling and putting on plays all the time. My Area is at the opposite end of the school. It's probably the quietest one, but it's still noisy so I just sit and watch and talk and laze about during the day, and do all my writing at night. Most of the teachers are real friendly though, and they're always talking about interesting things or showing films or bringing speakers in. And they're not always on your back like they were at my last school. They want you to have your own opinions and to choose work that interests you. That's good, I reckon. It's like being treated like an adult. But the school's still crazy. It's filthy and wrecked, and lets crazy kids get away with anything.

Wednesday March 4th

No kidding, if you took any notice of Billy, you'd reckon everyone in the world who wasn't like him was a poofta. He's this kid at school who's always looking at his ugly face in the dunny's mirrors, trying to get the best out of his pimples and rotting teeth.

"You should have seen the brawl, mate." He was so excited when he was telling me that he kept shoving me and his eyes were flashing everywhere. "This big fat guy was trying to pull out of the kerb when he hit the side of this hotted-up old Holden. A young guy with a peaked-cap on got out, rushed back, dragged the fat guy out, and laid him out on the road with one punch. No kidding, just one punch," he said, showing me how the punch was thrown. "When they picked him up, he had blood all over his face and down his shirt, and the silly poofta was crying. And while he got down on the ground and started feeling around for his smashed glasses, the other guy's mother came up and started screaming at him too for hitting her son's car. When I left, the tow-truck drivers were all over him while he was still looking for his glasses. What a goose. You should have seen it, mate."

Even while I was listening, I was surprised that I was almost shaking with anger. Why punch the fat guy? It was only an accident. Billy was always telling me those sorts of stories, like it made him tough or something. And he's always calling me *mate* as if we're close friends. I get the feeling he thinks I'm a poofta too, and is protecting me. He

11

can't keep still he's so nervous, and is always showing off. I don't know why the girls go for him; it must be the smooth way he talks to them, like he's been around a lot. I reckon I only have one real close friend at school, and that's Charlie. Billy doesn't seem to like me being Charlie's friend, and always calls him a poofta too. Charlie just ignores it. He knows he can beat Billy, I reckon.

Thursday March 5th

The first time I saw that old Cypress tree, I was filled with respect for it. It looked magical, like the 'Faraway Tree' I read about years ago; like one of those old knotty teachers you come across, and you'd feel embarrassed to muck around in front of them, like they're your dead grandparents or something. Anyway the first time I saw this tree, I was dopey from tiredness, squeezed between boxes of books and ten million coathangers, half-lying, half-propped up on this Tibetan carpet in the back of our station-wagon.

Alec switched to high-beam on the headlights, and there in front of us was this huge ghostly tree that made the house and car seem tiny. It was as if it ran the place, peering down over everything and not looking too happy about having the strong light shone in its eyes. Alec had said something about how were we going to celebrate our arrival. Jackie wanted to sing 'We're here because we're here'. Andy hadn't even stirred on her lap and I was only semi-conscious.

I saw Mum and Dad's heads silhouetted as they came together in a kiss in the front seat. Then Alec leaned over to me and said: "What do you say, mate, we start unpacking?"

I remember just smiling weakly back at him in the dark. It was going to be a while before I had my first sleep in our new house. Alec had turned out the headlights, and just like magic, the Cypress, like an enormous cathedral, had vanished into the night.

It was last August that we moved into this house.

Friday March 6th

I don't think anything scares my little brother, although he hates being in the bedroom alone with the light off. He lies on his side, all bleary-eyed waiting for me to come to bed, and when he sees me getting undressed he usually falls straight to sleep. I played a trick on him once. I set up clothes and objects all around the room and went to bed with a torch.

"You awake Andy?" I said. "Look at this."

And I shone the torch on hanging coats and objects, and they looked like monsters and mutilated corpses. He gave a tired laugh and started to snore.

I reckon he and Alec have a lot in common. They are always heading off outside together, and even though they go their own ways to do things, they always seem to be pretty close. The ways Andy behaves would be just how Alec would have mucked around when he was a kid. I mean roller-skating and footy and stuff just don't seem to be their scene.

Monday March 9th

"Have a go at describing yourself," Paul Kelly said.

Jackie reckons I'm lanky with a baby-face which makes me good looking. Alec reckons I'm too serious. People think if you don't laugh out loud and roll on the ground holding your side, then you don't have a sense of humour. I laugh a lot to myself on the inside. Sometimes Paul Kelly points a finger at me in front of the class and says: "Caught you smiling." Andy calls me 'ghost-face' when he wants to annoy me. I do have a white face which makes the freckles around my nose stand out.

People also reckon you've got to show off to prove just how smart or tough you are. I know I'm smart; I'm not ordinary, so don't have to prove it to anyone. I like to watch people doing dumb things all around me, and try and work it out inside. That's why I'm happy just to have one or two friends. It gives me more time to sit and watch.

Paul Kelly's written about three times on my work: "Mark, you could have done better here. I know you have an imagination, but you rarely seem to want to share it."

Why should I? Just because my dad's a teacher at the same school? I'll only share things like that when I reckon I need to and people deserve it.

Some kids call me things like 'goodie-goodie' and 'snob', just because I don't have long hair and act tough. Let them. Who needs them?

Tuesday March 10th

I want to tell you how we started on the place after moving in. From the moment he saw it, Alec said he loved this house.

"It's old and warm and friendly," he said smiling at us. "It reminds me of going to visit your grandparents, and being given lollies and lemonade and eating fruit off their trees until your guts ached."

He also said it gave out vibes of not being treated properly by previous owners, and it needed love and care to bring it back to good health. You didn't need to feel vibes to know that; you could see that it was really knocked about and that there was junk everywhere. When he talks about vibes, Jackie pulls this face and looks up as if there's a porn film being shown on the ceiling.

So from the start we were ripping up old lino, replacing broken windows, cleaning out dead birds from behind the boarded-up open fireplaces, and scrubbing toilet-bowls and basins that were a shitty brown and green. Jackie and Alec said that there were years of work to be done, but that the house was livable-in right then. Andy and I agreed; it was like an adventure of living in a farm-house, even if it was in an inner-suburb.

Alec wanted to start on the garden first. He reckoned that to complete a garden took years and years, because that's how long it took trees and shrubs to grow. He said if we finished that work first, then the garden would work on itself by just growing, but if we did the house first, then we wouldn't have shade trees and fruit trees and vegetables and plants with beautiful native flowers and smells for a long time – and who could wait that long. It was hard to argue with that. We all had a say about what went on in the house, as if it was a school Area meeting; it's just that it would have seemed silly to go ahead with something Alec didn't agree with, almost that it wouldn't work for sure. We went outside and stared at the long thick grass which had old pipes, metal, toys, broken bottles, clothing, bricks, lino and concrete all tangled up in it. Then there was the mountain of rubbish we had brought out from the house, and a huge area of concrete just outside the back door that Alec said would have to be smashed up.

Anyway we decided to start the job by conning as many of our friends to come and help on the Saturday, and for helping we provided them with a sheep-roast (you know, how the Greeks do it, on a spit covered with tomato-paste and garlic and stuff), and plenty to drink. It started to piss with rain just as they arrived, but it stopped no one; everybody worked their guts out for about six hours straight. About ten people worked on smashing up the concrete and throwing it in the eight-tonne bin in the sideway that had been hired. Andy must have thought he was the foreman on that job the way he carried on. He loved using the sledge-hammer, and no one could get it off him.

In the meantime one of Alec's friends, Alfredo, had dug a

15

pit under the clothes-line and had cooked the sheep, rigging some old roofing-iron and cardboard over the line to keep things dry. And we had loud music going all the time and even though it was hard work, it was also like a party. People kept coming and going and doing their little bit. So when it started to get dark we all slumped around the fire which had been built up into a bonfire; and we ate the sheep, and it stopped raining completely, and then flagons of wine were drunk, and there were two guitars being played, and everyone was exhausted but real happy and drunk, and it was like we were in the bush because the air was so cool and clean from the rain.

Andy and me were the first up in the morning just to see what had been done in daylight. All around the back door was a mess of clay mud and water. Beer and wine bottles stood around like those garden-gnomes you see in Italian nurseries. But the concrete had gone, and already the yard seemed bigger. We had left a path of concrete leading down to the back of the yard, and the concrete in the driveway was still intact, and that surrounded the Cypress to the bottom of its trunk. And that huge pile of rubbish that we had learnt to live with had gone. Andy and I walked down to where the pit had been dug. Chairs still sat around it as did empty and half-empty scattered glasses. The coals were still warm so we threw any leftovers on it and in no time had the fire going again.

It was good sitting around it on that cool, quiet Sunday morning. Just occasionally I got flashes of the most hectic moments of the day before. Without saying anything, Andy went into the house and came out with a couple of bowls of muesli, and as we sat in the silence munching away, we sort of tingled with the excitement that we had made a start and also felt so shagged. The muscles in my hands and thighs and back were stiff.

Alec and Jackie staggered out about 11:00am, Alec looking real ratshit, and by the amount of orange juice Jackie drank, I figured she wasn't that great either. We were all pleased and we were a family. Alec looked at the compost-heap that then was nearly three weeks old and which was only about three metres from the pit. He started to laugh to himself.

"What?" Andy said.

"I fell into that last night," Alec said. "And when I looked up, Alfredo and Mike were just staring at me. I told them to help me out before I was eaten by the worms and slaters, but they were too far gone even to stand."

Alfredo and Mike staggered out of the lounge after mid-day and ate a dozen oranges each, then finished off everything in the fridge.

Wednesday March 11th

There's nothing worse than the first period after lunch. It's hard enough trying to eat your lunch and drink a can of Coke while playing a footy match, but before you know it, time is up, and you've got to go and sit in the classroom, and your body is throbbing with heat and you can feel the sweat on the back of your legs and shirt and in your socks, and your face is burning, and you try and write with your biro, but it just keeps slipping out between your fingers, and all you want is a drink, and you promise yourself the next day you'll knock off footy earlier to cool down, but you never do.

Thursday March 12th

This stray dog wandered into our place this afternoon as if he had always lived here. Jackie was coming in from the backyard, and when she opened the glass-door of the sun-room, he just trotted in and lay on the rug. She reckoned the dog gave her that look which meant it hadn't had a decent meal for years. Andy seemed the only one to know him.

"You here again," he spluttered over our visitor, patting him on the chest and rubbing behind his ear. The dog licked everyone's wrists as if he was signing on board. Alec gave us a lecture about the responsibilities of keeping a dog, and Jackie said it would cost a bit to keep him, but you can tell from their eyes and tone of voices that they like our visitor too.

Friday March 13th

The dog was still here when I got home from school. He slept on an old couch in the garage, to judge by the circle of hair on it. When I got up this morning he was snooping around the backyard, checking out the trees and vegetables and chooks and their coop and anything else that might have a scent. He didn't seem to take any notice of the four of us standing there watching, Jackie with some tea in her hand, Alec pulling at some couch-grass among the vegetables.

Sunday March 15th

Yesterday morning it was Jackie's and my turn to do the shopping at the market. I always feel good wandering up and down the stalls with her looking for bargains. It's more a game than a necessity. I feel good about it because it is one time during the week we get out just together and talk and laugh a lot. And it's good because there are always the same guys falling over backwards to try and con her on because she's real good looking and doesn't wear a bra and sometimes no shoes, and when they say real flirty things to her, they're looking sideways at their mates as if they're doing well with her, and she always stops and has a joke with them

18

and buys some fruit or vegetables and gives me the same glance as they give each other, as if she's playing the same game and I'm her mate. And they always ask the same dumb question, whether I am her boyfriend, and she always says the same thing which is "Maybe", and I usually score a free apple or something for not saying anything because I'm watching real close what's going on and I bet they play the same games even if Alec is there, except then they probably say is he her father or something dumb like that.

Yesterday morning we got to the stall where we usually buy half a case of oranges which I usually have to lug back to the car. An Italian guy and his son own the stall. There was a crowd hanging around dangling one-dollar notes because you get twenty small navels for a dollar. Anyway, would you believe it, but right in the middle of the son pushing out his great hairy chest and arms from a black singlet, Jackie farted real loudly. Everyone around went quiet and pretended nothing had happened; but the son's chest and shoulders sank.

"You shouldn't have done that," I said as we moved away. "It was embarrassing."

"Bullshit," she said. "What do you mean 'done it'? No one can help farting; they just slip out. It's natural. And anyway, the loud ones don't smell."

"You could have held it in," I said.

"Don't be silly." She sounded impatient, and walked ahead to the delicatessen section.

Monday March 16th

I'm supposed to have scored a girlfriend today. This girl, Cathy Roussos, reckons she's been rapt in me since the beginning of the year. She's tall with brown wavy hair and dark eyes, and she gets a few pimples. I reckon the only times I've spoken to her this year were when she took my ruler without asking.

So today in the canteen, Rosie, her girlfriend, came up to Billy and me, and asked Billy if Cathy and me were going together.

Billy sort of started acting like my manager and said to Rosie: "Maybe. Does she want to go with Mark?"

And Rosie said: "Maybe. Does Mark want to go with her?"

Billy said: "Maybe."

When she walked away, Billy turned around with a big smile on his mug, and bashed me on the arm.

"You're in. You've scored," he said, watching over his shoulder to see if he was being recognised as my manager. So I'm sort of going with Cathy. She's got a nice smile, and she's the first girl I've gone with at this school. Not that I care if I go with girls or not.

Tuesday March 17th

My brother's not considered the brightest kid at his school; in fact if you read his report cards you would find comments like, "a little slow", "lacks motivation", "possibly has remedial problems", "sleepy", "doesn't participate", "daydreamer", "disturbs the other children with uncustomary behaviour". We went along as a family to pick up these reports, and Jackie would look concerned and hold the teacher's hand, while Alec would sit there and smile to himself as if he was proud of the reports. I never knew why I was dragged along, and Andy would sit there with his eyes rolled up in his head or grab the opportunity to slip away and take a fire-extinguisher apart in some dark corner.

Jackie always said the same thing in the car on the way home: "We've been too permissive, Alec."

And Alec would put one hand on her shoulder and laugh.

"He'll learn to read and write when he feels a need for it," he'd say.

That seemed to be the big problem. Andy can hardly read

or write, and he's eleven. I always wanted to be able to read and write and Alec and Jackie have helped me for as long as I can remember. The trouble with Andy is that he prefers just to listen. He loves to be read to, as if he can see what's going on better that way. He also likes large books with glossy pictures of animals and insects and birds and plants and primitive tribes. But probably what he loves most is this dumb record Dad has had since he was a kid. It's a story about how the Lone Ranger finds his horse Silver. No kidding, I reckon he's listened to that record a million times.

For the rest of the time he's in his own world, which is either inventing or destroying. He just moves around the world pulling things apart and putting them back together again. Once I was really going to smash him for taking a part out of the TV, but Alec said to leave him alone because one day he might want to be a TV repair-man.

I have to admit it though, he is pretty clever with his hands. We all rely on him to fix things around the house no one else can do. And he takes on jobs as if he's been in the business for fifty years. Yet it's a funny thing; when he writes his hand is all shaky, but when he fixes things – no worries. And it's only when he has some homework to do that he needs his asthma inhaler.

I bet the other kids at school don't call him dopey though, because even though he's a little plump (baby fat, Jackie calls it,) there'd be no point in trying to pick on him because he can't read or write because he just wouldn't bloody listen.

Wednesday March 18th

This stray dog has got some pretty crazy habits. I was out in the yard on Saturday cleaning my runners so that they could dry in the sun, when he comes sniffing around me and before I realised it, he had lapped up a bottle of white shoe-cleaner. If he turns white I'll know the secret. He's one of those dogs that can give you filthy looks out of the side of his eyes; and sometimes when the side of his lip gets caught up over a tooth, you'd reckon he's sneering or laughing at you. Dogs are great.

Thursday March 19th

Other kids' mums are kinda different. They get fat real young with loose fleshy arms and they have big arses, and wear daggy dresses and get their hair cut short and spend most of their time cleaning up after you and fighting dirt and germs so that their house is seen to look good and their family is safe from diseases. They're all nice and friendly, but they always look tired, and like they've misplaced something or lost it or trying to remember something.

Jackie is different. Her long brown hair is bouncy and it makes her face look young; and when she walks, she almost runs because she's tall and athletic. If she's sitting in a lounge-chair, she rests her legs over the arms and shows off her hairy legs. I remember once when Andy and me were watching her do her yoga and she only had her knickers on; I could see little lines like scars running down the bottom of her stomach.

"What're those?" I asked, and Andy also leaned a little closer for a look.

"You put them there," she said. "That's where my tummy stretched when you were inside me."

"Oh," I said, feeling kind of guilty.

"You were a real little terrier," she said, rolling her legs back over her head and touching the floor. "Even then I could tell you were going to like football. You were doing punt kicks and back-flips when I was just five months pregnant. Don't you remember?"

"No," I said, feeling even more guilty.

She laughed as her legs came back down. "You made life

exciting. Alec and I used to lie in bed watching you move around, and it seemed impossible to imagine that something so large was growing inside of me and was going to want to come out . . . I could hardly wait."

"You had me when you were real young didn't you?" I asked.

She was doing this thing called the Cobra, so her voice was strained because her neck was stretching. "You were an accident, mate, and so here you are; my strapping fourteen year old wonder boy."

I think she was just softening me up after calling me an accident. Then she went down on her knees, pointed at her forehead, and then stood on her head. Andy went down on his knees also and turned his face upside down to talk to her.

"What about me?" he sort of spluttered into her face which was growing red from the blood rushing into it.

"Yes, you were a bit of an accident too," giving him an upside down wink, "but don't tell Alec . . . a sneaky one."

"What was I like inside you?" he said seriously, as if she hadn't understood him.

"Quiet as a mouse," Jackie said, coming down and resting her head on her fists on top of each other on the floor. "I would say you just swam around for nine months as happy as Larry. In fact I was surprised that you weren't born with flippers on."

Andy stared at her: "Get away." And then looked again at the lines on her stomach. "Did I do them too?"

"Yep," she said, and he looked around at me real proudly, even though his nose was running a little from the cold.

And I'll tell you, Jackie doesn't care much about dirt and germs either. She reckons that's why your body's there, to take care of them. Our house is always messy because everyone who lives in it is messy. About once a month we all have a clean-up, and take it in turns to do different jobs. When it's all finished you can find everything you thought you lost and you roll around on the floor without sucking up dust; and I reckon if your house was always clean and you were always cleaning up, then you would miss out on that excitement.

Friday March 20th

Friday afternoon at school is activities time. I usually go roller-skating with Charlie and Billy. All of a sudden Cathy Roussos is going too. Even though I'm supposed to be going with her, we've still hardly talked. Yesterday at lunchtime I stood up close next to her in the canteen with a whole bunch of other kids, but nothing's really happened – until today.

There's this cloak-room at skating which is never used any more; but the door's never locked. Billy reckons some kids meet in there to have sex. Today he skated up to me and said with that stupid great smile and rotting teeth: "Rosie said Cathy'll meet you in the cloak-room."

He had already accepted for me, so I didn't have any choice. I waited until the teachers and owner weren't looking, and sneaked into the room. I bumped straight into her in the dark. We kissed, and she kept on making these dumb moaning noises. I guessed I was supposed to touch her breast, and when I did, she put her hand over mine real tight, like she was trying to break my knuckles. I didn't have a clue what it meant – except maybe she didn't want me to put my hand anywhere else. All I had was a handful of her jumper and a squashy bra.

"We'd better go," she said in the dark, and I saw her silhouette slip out the door. Jesus, I thought; I'll have to go out and listen to Billy crap on.

Paul Kelly won't be reading today's entry in my diary. Some things I'm going to put aside. That's fair. Cathy's father would kill me I reckon if he knew what happened today. Greeks are real strict with their daughters.

It was one of those shit-house days when the last thing you want to do is visit relations you couldn't give a stuff about. I mean their kids reckon they own everything and all you want to do is punch someone in the face or leave as soon as possible. They live in the hills past Dandenong, and on the way there, Alec had been on about how he used to go there as a kid. He raved on about how it used to be a whole day's trip in his father's old Chev, and his family had to stop every couple of hours to let someone out to have a piss behind a gum tree.

I sat in the back of the Wagon on the way (even though I had tried every trick to get out of going), and Alec and Jackie were in the front and Alec had Andy next to him letting him steer the car. He was stuck up there real proud like he's some world champion racing-driver, and I was stuck in the back by myself playing with old butts in the ash-tray and wondering whether I should make a jump for it. I'm not asked if I want to have a go at steering . . . like I'm at the age where I might take over completely and start using the accelerator and clutch . . . not that I wanted to play the dumb game anyway.

Jackie gets the shits when Alec lets Andy steer. She reckons it's an unnecessary risk and that he isn't being responsible. I agree too. She didn't say anything but you could tell she was close to jumping down his throat. Andy just smiled away in the rear-vision mirror. This time I wanted to show them just how bored they were making me, so I leaned over the front seat and turned the radio on up loud to drown myself in some music. Alec didn't even give it a chance. He turned it right down without even asking me. He said when you're in the countryside the last thing you want is noise pollution. Jesus . . . I looked around . . . We were on the bloody Mulgrave Freeway.

Jackie had snapped at him: "Don't come that noise pollution bullshit when you're risking all our necks."

And they really started to argue about each other being bullshit artists, so I leaned over and turned the radio up loud again, which only made Alec angrier. They kept arguing and picking on each other's faults . . . like he reckons she smokes too much and will get lung cancer . . . and she reckons he spends his whole life telling other people how to run theirs. I tried to ignore them by concentrating on the music but I couldn't hear it because of all the noise pollution in the car. And when I looked into the rear-vision mirror, Andy's face showed that his mind was on Mt. Panorama at Bathurst. His back was dead straight.

This noise pollution shit gets me angry too . . . especially when I remember how it was used as an excuse not to let me go halves in a trail-bike with Charlie. Anyway it turned out a rotten day. Jackie and Alec wouldn't forgive each other, even on the way home. I felt glad when we had got home that it was a lousy day because they had no right to make me go in the first place. It's a waste of a good Sunday . . . and Jesus, I'm fourteen, I don't want to be dragged around like a kid.

Monday March 23rd

All weekend, Andy was doing his 'I know something you don't' act. He bows his head a bit, and looks up through the top of his eyes and smirks. If I ignore him long enough, he'll tell me, or he sings to himself that he knows something real important. He had been carrying on like this right up until before tea tonight; so when Alec and Jackie went out to take the clothes off the line together, I trapped him in the bedroom. He said he didn't know anything, so I pinned him down on the bed with my knees on his arms and gave him the slag torture – that's where you let some saliva slowly hang down towards the other person's face, and then suck it in quickly just before it drops off.

"Get off me, you big shit," he moaned and laughed and

26

wriggled.

"Tell me then," I said quietly.

"No . . . No . . . Don't you slag on me . . . Don't, Mark, you're hurting my arms . . . I don't know anything . . . all right I'll tell you . . . No, no, don't . . . I'll tell you; Dad's got a girlfriend."

"What do you mean?" I laughed.

"Austin told me," he said.

"Who in the hell's Austin?"

"This kid at school . . . Get off me will ya . . . Dad teaches his sister . . . Ow . . . Don't, don't . . . She reckons there's this girl who's in love with Dad."

I waited, but he stopped and lay still which meant it was the end.

"Is that all?" I said, sucking in the saliva, and feeling disappointed for having wasted all that energy.

When you think about it, he talks funny. I mean I mumble and talk too fast and forget real easy words, making it hard to finish a joke – but he's a splatterer. He talks quietly and muffled and spits when he gets excited as if his tongue was like a lump of wet football bladder rubber that was always getting in the way. If he gets excited at the table, you're liable to get a soggy crust or piece of potato spat over your eyeballs. When he talks to himself though, he usually sounds all right. Who knows, one day he might have a big chest, and stand on stage with big horns on his head and sing opera and be famous.

Andy can be pretty generous though. He makes little things and leaves them as gifts in places for you to find them – like your pocket or under your pillow, that sort of stuff. He made Jackie some perfume recently by soaking lemon leaves and some herbs in water. She found it in her bedroom. It was in a vinegar bottle. There's one thing you'll never get him to share though, and that's his sandwiches. He's a sandwich freak; he is always making them, and I'll tell you what, some of the things in his sandwiches I would not go near.

Billy showed me this old pencil case he flogged from some other kid's locker today. He was all excited and trying to keep his voice down at the same time. You should have seen his eyes . . . they were alight and his voice was stuttery as he told me how he 'found' it in 'this sucker's locker'. I just couldn't see how an old pencil case was worth stealing, but then what's that make me, some big time crook who only robs banks for a million dollars?

Billy's always stealing things, like he's got some sort of sickness. And he's got this strange idea of who owns what. Once a teacher caught him with a blackboard marker. Now the only people who own them are teachers.

"Where did you get that, Billy?" she asked.

"I found it," he said real aggressively.

"Well I'll have it now," she said. "I could use one of those." I reckon she was trying her hardest not to accuse him of stealing.

Anyway he held it real tight behind his back as if it was a matter of life and death.

"No way," he said when she put her hand out. "This is mine . . . I found it." And he was nearly crying and looking like he was going to go bananas. "You can't take it off me . . . I found . . . it's mine."

"Oh well, perhaps sometime you'd like to give it to me as a gift," she said, going back to her teaching.

"Maybe," he had said, looking suspiciously around him, as if someone might be trying to sneak up behind him.

Billy's got this idea that as soon as you put something down, you don't own it any more, even if it's got your name on it.

"No way," he would say. "You shouldn't have put it

28

down." A lot of kids are like that . . . especially with pens. Someone flogged my pen so I'm flogging yours. That's the rule.

But the crazy thing about Billy is that it's almost as if he wants to get caught. He's always handing hints around, and almost tells the teachers. It's as if he wants to get into trouble and then get the third-degree from some teacher. I just can't understand that, and he knows if his old man gets called up, he will get a bashing. He reckons he hates his old man because he's always out getting drunk and bashes his mum. And he hates his oldest brother because he's always getting bashed by him and he gives his mother a hard time too.

But I reckon there's nothing he wouldn't give you if you asked for it. Crazy.

Wednesday March 25th

I've just completed a scientific experiment; I tasted my own sperm. It's funny how much courage it took me – I suppose like the first time I pulled myself off; and pulling yourself takes a bit of planning too, especially when you're sharing a room with your little brother whose ears flap. I reckon I've eaten and drunk some pretty crazy things in my life, but you would have thought I was committing suicide tasting my sperm. I mean it wasn't that I had much, just a bit on my finger where it dribbled between my fingers. I screwed my face up at a slightly salty taste, but then I reckon I felt disappointed because not only was I still alive, but it didn't have much taste at all.

Funny about the whole thing. I sort of felt proud because I had done it, as if I had just passed some test about the human body. And lying there, I wondered if I would ever bother to do it again, and the thought of tasting someone else's sperm didn't seem too hot, and I wondered what the other kids were on about at school when they got all excited about getting a girl to swallow the lot. Who'd want to do that?

Alec walked into the sunroom tonight after closing the door like he was trying to wreck it.

"What happened?" Jackie asked.

"Nothing," he snapped. "Jesus, they're bloody hopeless."

He slumped down, and when nobody said anything, he seemed to decide to have a gripe. "We had one of those bloody staff-meetings again. Jesus Christ, I had this girl at Recess-time crying her heart out because her step-father's been trying to get at her. Christ almighty, do you know what? She sleeps and showers with her clothes on. And she was so afraid I might go to the police because he's the only family she's got."

He got up after just sitting down, and started walking around real tense and yelling at Jackie as if it was her fault. "And all they can talk about is bloody yard-duty rosters and where we'll go at the end of the year for the staff break-up. It's like they're afraid to face up to the real problems all around them."

He sat down again as if he had run out of things to say. He stared at his hand, and said quietly: "We're just a collection of rather ordinary people with ordinary ideals; afraid of over-involvement, and afraid to ask ourselves how effective we are as teachers."

He looked at Jackie, took a deep breath and smiled: "Except for a few suckers who have to do the lot."

Jeez, he takes his job seriously.

Friday March 27th

I suppose Charlie is my best friend at school because we like

30

a lot of the same things – and he doesn't hassle me like Billy does. Sometimes he gives me the shits though, like today. During Home-group meetings yesterday morning, Paul Kelly had wanted to know who would prefer to go and see this dumb film instead of the usual roller-skating. Most of the kids reckoned they wanted to see the film. I had already seen the previews, and anyway we only had skating once a week, and Cathy might be there. Charlie said he didn't know what to do.

"Don't go to the film," I said to him. "It's dumb. Come roller-skating."

He said right-o, but I couldn't talk any of the other sucks out of going to see the film. If there weren't enough kids going roller-skating, then it would be cancelled for the week. With Charlie and me, there were eight altogether, just the right number.

This morning, would you believe it, Charlie turns up with his money to go to the film.

"Changed my mind," he said going off with Billy to the canteen.

Jesus, I thought. What sort of loyalty is that from your best friend? In the end roller-skating had to be called off, and I spent the afternoon back at school doing boring Maths and English exercises from some dumb book which was too easy anyway. If I had known, I would have gone to the film too. I was in a foul mood by the end of the afternoon.

On the way home, I saw Paul Kelly and the kids from the film walking back from the tram-stop.

"You should have come. It was a great film, mate," says Charlie as if he's a stranger.

I felt sick. I knew also they wouldn't have to do the extra English and Maths I had done. It was like punishing some-one for standing up for their principles.

"What's up, comrade?" said Alec, taking a can of beer out of the fridge. I told him.

"He doesn't have to do what you tell him to do. That

doesn't make a good friend, does it, Mark?" said Alec.

"I'm not saying he has to," I said, and my voice sounded kind of young. "But he said he was going skating, and then he let down all the kids who were going and the whole thing was called off."

"So he changed his mind – that's okay, isn't it?" Alec let out a loud belch.

"Well, why did he say he was going in the first place, then?"

Alec looked straight at me.

"No one has the right to own someone else, especially a friend," he said.

"Who said anything about wanting to own him?" I replied angrily. "And anyway, what about me? You own me, don't you? I'm your son; I'm your bit of property."

"Do I?"

"Of course you do," I shouted.

"Then if you feel as if you're owned by me," he said slowly and a little sad, "and I've made you feel that way, then I'm ashamed."

"Well who pays for my education – and for my clothes – and food – and pocket money – and roller-skating – and who owns the house and the car and the TV?" I knew my last argument was going to be the best. "And anyway, don't you want to own me? Don't you want me to be your son?"

Andy, the little smart-arse, was having a chuckle to himself, as he was spreading some sort of weird vegemite and honey sandwich.

"No, I don't," Alec said, smiling. "I love you as a person, for all the things that make up you."

"But I'm part of you," I answered. "You had me, didn't you?"

Alec thought for a moment.

"When you want to own someone," he said, "it's usually because you don't want to see them change. You enjoy them as they are. But human beings, given the chance, like to go

32

through changes; to discover new feelings, and experience new things – and people. It seems pretty natural to me; and no one has the right to try and stop them because they reckon they own them. They haven't got a friend any more; they've got a prisoner."

"But most people tell others what to do," I said butting in.

He put both of his palms up in the air as if he was lifting the world.

"There are prisoners all around us," he said.

"But what about Jackie?" I said. "She always does what you want to do."

This didn't seem to impress him because he didn't say anything more. He didn't even smirk this time. He got up, finished the can, and walked out.

Saturday March 28th

Uncle Liam dropped in this afternoon on the way to the pub. He's not really my uncle; he calls himself Uncle Liam, so everyone else does. He's a guy who lives three doors down, and sometimes drops in for a beer with Alec. Funny, you never see hardly anything of his wife, not even in the street; but he is well known, walking down the street, sometimes staggering a little, the old kit-bag swinging at his side. And when he sees you, he lifts his hand in a strange wave, as if he's throwing a magic net over you to protect you, or like one of those priests splashing water everywhere. Alec always gets out a couple of bottles while Uncle Liam goes through his bag looking for gifts he sometimes carries, like a chicken or some lollies.

"And there's me favourite wee-fella," he calls Andy, shaking his hand as if he's making some sort of deal with another man. And then he will put his hand up as if he is swearing on the Bible, and will say with a very serious look: "This wee-fella will be the greatest of them all one day."

And then he laughs again as if he's the only one who knows where he got that information from.

He rolls cigarettes with tobacco that looks hundreds of years old, that he carries in a tin I've never seen before. And he always begins talking about the 'hills' where he was born in Ireland. The same stories over and over again.

"Did I tell ya about the lassie with the golden hair I met in the hills long ago?" he said to me today looking serious.

"No," I lied.

"Well, there you are," he said, and so started telling us about the time he was digging potatoes in the hills as a young man, when this girl appeared from nowhere. He reckons she was sent by the devil to get him.

"It's too late," he said to her. "I can see through the fire-coals in your eyes that you're on a mission of the Master." And so her eyes turned to ice, and next moment she was gone.

Since then, he reckons, he has spent his life fighting against the Queer Fella, which is what he calls the devil. He says the Masons are the ones being sent by the devil to get him, and that he is always in a war of wills against them. While he talks to you, he leans up real close, like twenty centimetres from your face; and you get a good view of his bloodshot watery eyes and the dry nicotine line on his lip on account of the fact he never takes the cigarette out while he's talking.

Andy will sit next to him right up close listening with his mouth open, his eyes wide, never saying anything, and Uncle Liam occasionally gives him a hug and laughs. Alec smiles to himself a lot and also keeps pretty quiet, like he thinks there's magic in him or something. Jackie never looks too impressed. She goes and does something else.

"And I'll tell ya another thing," he said to me about a month ago when he was looking around the vegetable garden. "Ya see that big tree there, the Cypress?"

He leaned right forward close to Andy and me who were the only ones with him: "That tree is like the Queer Fella.

34

It's a dying Spirit." And then he hugged Andy. "And only a wee innocent can release it."

.

Monday March 30th

It's funny but when Charlie acted like my friend again this morning, I forgot all about last Friday. Sometimes we hang around each other's places for tea and listen to records and talk. His parents are great. They're Italian and have a house that looks like a funeral parlour inside. It has a whole lot of statues and vases and things like that. And it looks modern with different wall-paper in each room. His dad makes his own wine and we drink it with our meals while he tells stories about the war and living on a farm in Sicily. He always gives Charlie and me a big squeeze which nearly kills us because he's short and fat and has huge hands and hair all over his body. His mum is fat also and she is always making these enormous meals especially for me which I can only eat half of. She always wants to know how Alec and Jackie and Andy are, even though she's never met them, and sends me home with food for them, usually cakes and chocolate-coated lollies. Charlie also has two sisters; one who's married and lives in Adelaide, and another one who is seventeen and looks beautiful and is a dental nurse.

Charlie's got this fantastic record collection, and we spend hours in his room doing our homework. He doesn't talk much and seems pretty serious, but when he mucks around, he goes mental and throws pillows and record covers at me. He doesn't really go out of his way to make friends at school, like me, except the kids sort of respect him, like they wouldn't pick on him. He seems mature. Most of the time after school he works in his uncle's delicatessen. He calls himself a salami-pusher and reckons one day he's going to be a dope-addict and play in a band. I reckon he looks like one now. He's got black curly hair and a big nose and walks everywhere with his hands in his pockets. Anyway he writes better poetry than anyone in our Area, and probably the whole school, and is always reading books by this guy Ray Bradbury.

Alec was asking everyone tonight at tea if it was okay that some of his students came around for a party this Thursday night. He said he was convinced that they should celebrate the success of a play they have just finished putting on. I only know a few of the kids from his Area. They get around as if they're older and more sophisticated than other kids at the school. They're always putting on plays or trying to flog their own newspaper or selling tickets for a disco at lunchtime that they've organised themselves. Andy just had a grin. I bet he mucks around. Jackie said that she was looking forward to meeting the play group.

Tuesday March 31st

Billy rushed up to me after school tonight.

"Hey, Mark," he said with this real worried look on his face. "You still going with Cathy Roussos?"

"Why?"

"George's going around saying he touched her up in the Gym at lunchtime."

"Of course I'm not," I said, trying to act calm.

I bet some kids are going to be laughing at me. I knew that Billy would be trying to get me to bash George.

Wednesday April 1st

I reckon Jackie would have made a fantastic artist. Everywhere she goes around the house, she leaves doodles, whether it's on the shopping list or on the telephone message pad. But she likes to doodle real big, and she doesn't scribble or anything, but leaves long thick and thin lines that just curl on forever until there's a bird standing in some rushes or a woman's face in a crowd.

Once she said she would like to be an 'Illustrator' but probably would never get the chance. She was an Art teacher once, but she said she didn't like what schools made kids do, and anyway she had her own kids to look after. She reckons Alec left teaching for a year too, and they both just stayed home looking after me and doing what they wanted to do. She said Alec started to get restless and wanted to be a teacher again, which she couldn't understand. She reckons schools are too much like the Army, all they do is teach kids how to be aggressive. Anyway she's got it pretty good. She works on designing patterns for materials three days a week for this small firm around the corner. She has these things called silk-screens around the house everywhere. Not bad – three days a week. Most of the kids' mums at school are trying to bring up a hundred kids, and that's after getting home from the factory at 6:00pm at night.

Friday April 3rd

Holiday today. It's Easter. Right now I can hear Alec and Jackie moving around the house cleaning up after last night's party. I should be having breakfast, but I can't stand it when the kitchen's all sloppy.

Alec got the things ready for the party last night, just as if there were adults coming. He cut up some bread-sticks, had bowls of cabana and cheese ready, and potato crisps, and peanuts, and made some punch which I noticed he slipped some brandy into – just a little. As it turned out, the only things the kids ate were the crisps and nuts and they all went off and came back with king-sized bottles of Coke to drink. It didn't seem to worry Alec, in fact I reckon he probably expected it; he just wanted to do it so it didn't look like he was treating them like kids.

Some kids arrived early, driven here by their parents to the front door, mainly the Greek girls. It was difficult to know what to do with them, because Alec was still getting things ready and Jackie was getting dolled up, so Andy and me sat in the loungeroom with them, and they lit cigarettes and we ate all the peanuts we could find. We just sort of stared at each other across the room. None of them seemed to recognise me from school. Anyway after a while, the girls asked if they could put a tape on.

I was real cool and said: "Yeah, no worries."

I even showed them how to work the stereo. It was hard to work out which group was on the tape because it had been recorded so badly, and the girls turned the volume right up and the bass too, and the treble completely down. The floorboards were bouncing and one of the speakers was vibrating badly. Anyway the girls all stood in the middle of the room in a circle and had another cigarette.

Andy got up wheezing a little, his mouth stuffed with peanuts, and said to them: "You know that music . . . that's shit." Then he pissed off, probably to watch Jackie putting some eye make-up on.

"Is that your little brother?" one of the girls spoke to me.

"No, he's the dog."

They all looked at me as if I was some sort of criminal.

"He's real cute," said the same girl, and they all left for a walk to the milk-bar.

"Where's the guests?" said Alec coming in, and looking amazingly young and happy.

"Gone to the milk-bar."

If some arrived early, the rest arrived late, just in time to watch one of the early ones picked up by her dad. The late ones had walked all the way because they couldn't figure out the public transport, and anyway it was an adventure together. As soon as they arrived the girls immediately lit up cigarettes, while the boys went all over our place checking it out. Then they just stood around in the doorways getting in the way. The girls looked about eighteen with their incredible clothes and make-up on, and I thought the kids at our school were supposed to be poor. And yet they were just my age or one year older. The boys kept standing around against the walls, eating the rest of the crisps and saying embarrassingly dumb jokes. While the late girls went and rang some boy on the phone, the boys all went down to the milk-bar together to buy some Coke.

The door-bell went and two more girls arrived, and I could hear them in the hallway asking Alec where the phone was so that they could ring one of their dads because he was going to pick them up in ten minutes, and could he ask if they could stay a little longer, and could he drive them home. Anyway Jackie ended up doing the dirty work and talking for them on the phone.

I decided to wander about a bit and found that the party was getting going because the two late girls had slipped a bottle of sparkling pink wine into the kitchen, and were quickly trying to get pissed. Andy was in a corner playing with a plastic bag with some sort of lollies in it and chuckling to himself.

"See, I told you," he said, calling me over. "I told you Dad's got a girlfriend . . . and she's here tonight. I spied on two girls in the dunny. That's what they were talking about."

I punched him on the arm, and was going to punch the other one when I noticed that some of the girls I had said he was the dog to, were watching. The real dog, the stray dog, was wandering around between everyone's legs looking real important and conning food with that look that said we didn't feed him here and we also tortured him. Some other girls had just put on a worse tape than the first one, and were doing a little dance together in a corner, all lined up in a row, just as their hands holding their cigarettes were. Then the guys came back and discovered the pianola, so I had to show them how it worked – though it was hard to hear the rolls

39

because of the room jumping with the stereo at full blast. Anyway the boys didn't care. They just went ahead and got pissed on Coke and sang the lyrics together as loud as they could to annoy the girls who were listening to the tape that you couldn't understand.

And right in the middle of the room and noise, Alec and Jackie sat cross-legged on the floor talking to some kids. Two of them were the best looking girls I've seen. They looked real mature; even the way they held their glasses of punch and had their cigarettes held up in the air, like adults do when they smoke. Alec was even smoking and he hardly ever does. One of these girls was real old and sexy looking. She had long blonde hair and her tits really stuck out and she had no bra on. I noticed Jackie look at her sometimes as if she was in an art gallery or something. And this girl sat right up close to Alec as if she was teacher's pet. What really grabbed me, though, was the way she kept looking at him, not like a kid does, but how an adult would. Her name was Lesley Anherbrat some kid said, and I just sat on the end of the couch and stared at her off and on.

It seemed to me the longer last night went on, the more those kids seemed to think they owned our house. I mean they must have known their crumby tapes weren't doing the stereo any good; and when they talked to each other, they were screaming like they were still at school. And when they walked around the house they slammed doors a lot and picked things up without asking. They didn't just sit in chairs and cushions, they fell on them or pushed each other over onto them. I mean, Andy and me do it too, but it's our house; we wouldn't go around to their place and do it. Some of them even started to have a cushion fight, but other kids told them to cut it out and stop being juvenile.

Jackie was beginning to butt in a little too and organise kids to do things, like pick up spilled drinks and peanuts. They did it willingly enough. Some girls even went out and started doing dishes and making coffee. But I still couldn't cope with the noise of the pianola and stereo distortions, so I played a trick and turned the stereo down. No one seemed to notice, so then I turned it down a little more and discovered everyone stopped shouting so much. At times Alec looked a little disappointed, as if he expected something different of them. I think he was watching them, as if he was waiting for them to realise what they were doing.

I guess that sort of sums up what Alec's like. I reckon he'd be a really good teacher, always cracking jokes, treating kids as if they were equals; always full of stories which were underneath really a lesson. He says he loves to go to school each day, to his other family. He reckons he prefers being around kids rather than adults because they are more honest and open and interesting. He says he can also learn more from kids than adults because adults are too busy being scared. He thinks school should be a happy place, and that teachers and students should be friends and learn from each other because he reckons people only learn things that they want to and nothing can change that. The best way to learn, he says, is to discover something for yourself. He says that if adults keep yelling and grizzling at kids, the kids just get bored with that teacher, and then that teacher might as well go and find another job. That's fair enough, but I like the teachers who are a bit heavy too, you know, they hardly ever do their block, but when they do, everyone ducks for cover.

Anyway you can sure enough see that Alec's students see him as a friend. They ring him up, drop around, give him presents, and so do their parents. It's like sharing him really, and sometimes it's bloody annoying if you want to do something with him, but he has to go off visiting some kid's parents. I mean when he gets home, he should just be himself, but he sits around the kitchen-table and goes on about what happened at school as if he thinks we were all there and interested.

Anyway he seemed to trust them enough last night, even though they were taking over the place.

In the end, I headed for bed. The light was on, and Andy lay on his side, his eyes forcing themselves to stay open.

"You coming to bed soon?" he said with a weak voice.

I got undressed and turned the light out, and for a while lay listening to the party and thinking about how Alec's students weren't afraid to put their arms around him or rest their chins and hands on his knee. I must have dozed a little then, but awoke, and heard that the music was finished and there was whispering in the hallway. Alec was getting ready to drive the last kids home.

One voice, I think it was that girl Lesley, said: "I bet you must think us pigs the way some of them were mucking around."

I heard Alec laugh quietly, but I felt like yelling out: "Yeah, well why didn't you tell them yourself to behave and turn the stereo down."

Now sitting here this morning writing, I sort of realise that I didn't say anything either, and anyway nothing was harmed.

Sunday April 5th

Alec, Jackie and I watched this show on TV last night about Rape. I reckon the guy who made the show must have been a bit of a rapist himself, because all he was interested in was re-creating scenes where girls had been raped, and there was a whole lot of heavy breathing and looking over the shoulder going on. Anyway one of the things the show said was that most rapists were part of the family or uncles or friends, in other words, known by the girl or woman. They said even fathers could be rapists, and then they went on to tell you about all the ways to avoid rape, like don't walk about alone at night if you're a woman, and have dead-locks on your doors, and remember that any guy can be a rapist.

And that's when Jackie got all excited and started talking

about how unfair it was being a female in this world, and that women had no rights – like why didn't they have the right to go for a walk at night without the fear of being attacked.

Alec agreed that the whole thing was unfair, but said because there were rapists around, it was up to the woman to avoid getting into the position of being raped, for her own good.

Jackie got real angry, you know, right out of the blue, and said that was bullshit and that he really made her angry sometimes. She said: "Why should it be left up to the woman to protect herself? Why don't women have as much right to roam free as men? What do you think it's like spending your whole life aware that you could be raped and killed, just because you were unlucky enough to be born a female!"

I was going to tell them that Billy said girls like getting raped, but when I looked at Jackie's face, I dropped the idea. Alec tried to laugh off her anger.

"I agree the same human right of freedom isn't there, but until it changes, women are just going to have to learn to protect themselves," he said.

That got her even more angry, and she was nearly crying. She started talking about not knowing what was in the minds of those guys who bip their horns at you in the street or whistle or yell out. But she was so upset that she kept getting tied up with what she was saying, and she was looking at Alec as if he was the worst rapist in the world, and in the end she stopped talking and stormed out of the room and went to bed, slamming the bedroom door as hard as she could.

That left Alec and me just sitting there looking at each other. He smiled and shrugged his shoulders, but I got the feeling that he felt uncomfortable because he couldn't feel what she felt – and I felt the same, as if I had let her down. But why had she got so angry?

Anyway Alec put some Indian music on, and we worked

together, he on correcting kids' work from school, me catching up on some Maths so some other teacher could do what Alec was doing. A couple of times he got up and went into the bedroom, and I heard the discussion continuing and finally both of them were laughing. But I couldn't stop thinking about their discussion. I mean it seemed to me that they had been talking like real strangers.

Monday April 6th

Andy can be worth watching sometimes. He was the one who introduced five new members to our home last October.

I had noticed for a while how all of a sudden he'd become interested in cooking, sitting at the kitchen table watching Alec or Jackie prepare a meal. Occasionally he would ask some dumb question about the ways of cooking, and was particularly interested in preserving fruit and making jams and chutneys. He even began to cook parts of our evening meals. His favourite plaything was pumpkin, which he poured everything over, from sauces with melted cheese, seeds and nuts to some cross between a custard and a porridge. You wouldn't find me eating any of that stuff, but Jackie and Alec always seemed to enjoy theirs, probably because they felt sorry for him or didn't want to discourage him; and he just sat there with a look on his face as if he were conducting an experiment.

Anyway, one Friday he decided to have a 'Free-from-school' day. He had something on his mind because he was up early and playing around with the fridge and shopping-lists. At the top of the list was pumpkin. He loves pumpkins. He plays with them like a toy. He feels their weight and roughness, and gets a big thrill when one is cut open because of the difference in colour from inside and outside, and that dewy stuff from the flesh which he licks and the seeds which he will guts down straight away.

When I got home from school that afternoon, the kitchen table was packed with full bottles and jars. Andy and Jackie sat there, with Jackie helping Andy spell the names on the labels for the jars. Would you believe – 'Andy's Pumpkin Relish'; 'Andy's Pumpkin and Plum Jam'; 'Andy's Pumpkin, Parsley, and Grapefruit Special'; 'Andy's Pumpkin, Tomato, and Mint Spread', and others I can't remember now. I thought we'd be eating the muck for years.

The next morning, however, was Saturday, and he was up again early and I saw him packing the jars into boxes and Jackie putting a cardtable and chair into the back of the station-wagon. Off they went and ten minutes later she was back without him.

"Is he all set up?" said Alec, looking up from the paper and sucking on a cup of tea.

"His spelling is awful," she laughed, hugging Alec from the back.

It turned out the little bugger had gone off to flog his jars to the Saturday morning shoppers up the street.

I just had to see him in action. At first I just hung around on the other side of the street. He had the cardtable stuck up on the footpath with what must have been about a hundred jars on top, under, and around it. On the front of the table there were some large posters hanging. One said – 'I mad these'.

And there sure were customers, so I had to cross the road and have a closer look. Some looked like expert pumpkin-eaters, holding the jars up to the light and examining them, reading labels with glasses balanced on their noses. There were old ladies who looked jealous, and were questioning him about his recipes.

"How did you get it to set?" said one lady who must have been a hundred years old.

A couple of Vietnamese guys were taking a close look at the colour of his 'Pumpkin and Peanut Butter'. Some people looked like they just felt sorry for him as if he must have been a real case. I remember one guy smelling the paraffin-wax seal – you'd have to be dumb.

He arrived home after midday with fifty dollars and empty boxes. He shook hands with Jackie and then off again he went in a rush, this time with Alec. When they got back, there were Alec and Andy asking me to help them unload wood and chicken-wire and nails and stuff. By the end of that weekend, there was an enclosure and roost built for chickens.

One week later, these five chooks arrived by train and were met by Jackie and Andy at Flinders Street Station. A delivery van left sacks of wheat and pellets and straw. And soon we were eating fresh eggs for breakfast. Andy either just sat and watched them, or spent time taking scraps to them, or pulling choice bits of grass or leaves from veg-etables for them. To me, they always seemed to be bitching and squabbling about something, and they're real selfish bastards with each other.

"Whaddya think?" Andy had said to me.

"Great," I said. I didn't want to let him down.

"Will ya help me look after 'em?" he had asked.

"Sure," I said. "Where did you get the idea from?"

"When I climbed the Cypress. I saw half our neighbours had 'em."

Tuesday April 7th

It probably would have been good having a sister . . . I mean I reckon I'd know more about girls that way. Jackie's always ready to talk about girls and their bodies and I've seen hers lots of times. But just lately I feel there are things I'd like to ask about their behaviour . . . you know, things like – "How do you know if they're secretly rapt in you?" . . . and "Why do they act dumb when you know they're real smart?" Why do they?

46

Jeez, Easter went quick. The days are still warm, but the mornings are getting cold and the vegetables we planted in spring are nearly all finished. Alec has been real moody for a few days; since the party, I suppose. I reckon he gets tired from teaching sometimes. Tonight during tea he nearly snapped Andy's head off. Alec had been talking about this argument over a table-tennis table at school.

"Zoran asked me for a game at lunchtime," he said. "Then Muzzafer came up and wanted to play. Zoran whinged that he had asked me to play first, so Muzzafer, who said he had set up the table, proceeded to pull it down. We waited until he had finished, then we put it up again, so then Muzzafer jumped up on a table next to Zoran and kneed him in the stomach. The kid's crazy. I just did my block, and screamed at him to go home and get his parents. 'No worries,' he said, smiling, and walked off. Zoran told me that Muzzafer has broken three of his bats this year. I tell you, the kid's crazy."

"You did the right thing," said Jackie.

Alec shook his head. "Not at all," he said sharply. "I was totally ineffectual in losing my temper and threatening what doesn't worry him. I've seen him walk all over his parents." He stopped a moment and looked a little sad. "Zoran handled the situation far more tolerantly and intelligently than I did. He watched and waited, very aware of Muzzafer's unpredictability, waiting out the storm, taking a little punishment along the way, but getting his own way in the end. The rules of the game at school are little different from outside and around the flats where he lives. He's learnt to be cunning; to be able to estimate the strengths and weaknesses of the enemy to survive. It just saddens me that Zoran can't find peace from this world at school."

And that's where Andy said: "Dumb wog."

You could see Alec's eyes flashing. "And what about

Uncle Liam? He's Irish," he said, not screaming, but with this nasty soft voice. "And the family next door are Greeks; and the old lady across the road who's always sweeping her path, she's Lebanese. And Mark's friend, Charlie; he's Italian. And the three brothers who live over in the flats, they're Vietnamese. And Jackie's mother is Dutch. Are they all dumb wogs too?"

Andy's face was a little red.

"They're not," he said. "But that Muzzafer kid is."

I laughed, so he told the both of us to get out of his sight. He sure doesn't like that word 'wog'. He should hear it enough at school to get used to it. Even the immigrants call each other wogs. It doesn't make sense.

Friday April 10th

This kid from another school tried to pick a fight with me at skating today for no reason. He reckons I cut him off. He was smaller than me, but looked real mean.

"Come outside, ya poofta," he said to me.

"Why should I?" I said and kept skating. Anyway he kept skating past and calling me a chicken, and every time I looked, he and his mates were laughing at me.

Why should I have to fight him though? I didn't hate him or even want to hurt him. And nothing had happened. How come everybody wants to fight over nothing? And anyway I didn't want to fight because I wasn't angry and I would have got beaten up. It would take something important, like someone attacking Jackie or something like that, before I'd lose my block, and then I'd be scared I couldn't stop.

But what made me real angry was that I felt guilty and embarrassed for not fighting him, and I could feel my ears and neck burning. You know some kids at school talk about getting into fights every weekend, and they use bits of wood and kick other kids in the head and think that's great. I don't know whether to believe them or not.

Saturday April 11th

I remember how we got the garden finished here by last December, and you could see Alec just itching to start the plastering and painting inside – which meant bang would go our holidays. At that stage he was keeping the garden going; the rest of us reckoned we had the right to a rest. It was getting a bit boring too, and it was easy to miss out on a lot of things on the weekends.

I'll tell you something though, the work was worth it. Let me tell you what we've been eating from the garden. We've had a choice of zucchinis, tomatoes, egg-plant, capsicum, passionfruit, silver-beet, peas, pumpkins, sweetcorn, beet-root, cucumbers, rhubarb, carrots, parsnips, and right from the beginning Jackie planted a whole lot of herbs, plus strawberries. And that's not including all the fruit from the trees. There's nothing like eating fresh food, especially when you've had a hand in growing it. And we didn't use any sorts of sprays or chemicals at all – we reckon if the insects want some of the vegetables and fruit, we're willing to share as long as they're not too greedy.

And we dug a pit which is lined with bricks and sand and has glass-doors resting across the top of it. You'd reckon they were leading to an underground air-raid shelter. That's our compost bin; and together with only buying things in bottles and paper-bags that can be used later, we hardly have any rubbish that goes out in the bins on Sunday night. Makes you wonder how much rubbish there is in this world which isn't necessary. I tried to tell the kids at school about that during a class discussion, and I reckon some of them agreed.

To me, the garden was at its best on warm summer nights about 6:30pm onwards. Alec built this rough old table and benches out of bluestone pitches and planks, and we sat out there and had tea or a drink or talked – surrounded by the smells of all the vegetables which were over a metre high, and the sprinkler going making everything fresh, and thousands of tiny insects rising and falling with the spray, and the last bees for the day buzzing around your toes, and the spiders thinking of getting their webs out, and the clover grass was real nice between your toes even though it hadn't been cut for a few months, and the chooks watching on, getting fat from all the left-overs, and everything was real green. The trees were dotted with fruit. You could sit there all night, and I would be strumming away on my guitar that I was just beginning to learn, and Andy would be talking to himself, and Jackie taking deep Yoga breaths, and Alec would wander among all the green as if it was another family of his, and I had the feeling we'd all grow and die together and that included the vegetables and the chooks.

Sunday April 12th

I've just finished getting my pack ready for the Camp next week. Alec seemed really restless all through tea tonight, like his mind was a million miles away. In the end he went for a drive by himself. Jackie is reading this book to Andy that he got from the library about the sort of things that live around ponds. I'm going to write something quick about poetry because of what happened down the baths this afternoon.

Poetry seems to have a bad name, as if it smells or has VD. Some teachers take you for poetry in a way you know they don't like it themselves – or are even afraid of it. Teachers who love poetry will dig up fantastic ones for you to listen to, and will get you dying to have a turn at writing poems yourself – even if they're about the simplest of things, from eating an apple to closing your eyes and listening to the air.

Alec now and then writes a poem, sometimes right in the middle of tea or watching TV; and sometimes we have all written some together by taking it in turns to add the next line. Poetry is like a game. There are no rules to how you write it. It's just like saying how you feel, but in a way that sounds good. Andy says it's crap. "I'd rather *do* something," he says, whatever that means.

Anyway the reason I started writing about poetry is what I overheard in the dunnies at the baths. These two young guys had come in at first, and then another guy, and he sounded old but had a real warm feeling about his voice.

"Goodaye," said one of the younger voices.

"Howdie and a good day to you my friend," said the older one.

"Pretty warm for six o'clock at night in the middle of April," said the young guy in return with a hint of laughter in his voice.

"It's a beautiful night and day," said the old guy. "It's as if the day and night are one, as if it could be dawn, daybreak or noon . . . and inseparable."

"Yeah," said the third voice without thinking.

"It's like when I used to watch the tides," says the old guy. "At times you couldn't tell if it was ebbing, washing, or at growth. It was a moment of all together."

"Yeah," said that third voice again.

I got kind of excited and wanted to see this old guy. I pulled up my pants quickly, flushed, and opened the door. There were only two kids there, one giving the other a look that said an old drunk had just left them. I hurried out to the pool, but there were at least four older guys, old-men-of-the-sea types with paunchy bodies and white hair all over their shoulders and backs, getting their late swim in for the day. And I knew one of them was a poet.

Just got back from the Camp tonight. It went okay, until coming home. You should see some of those kids when we leave for a camp. Even before you leave, they sit up inside the bus eating crisps and lollies and drinking Coke, like it will be their last meal for a week. And they all have their transistors going at the same time, and they all want to sit in the same seat. I tell you, they're like babies.

And when you get out into the countryside, they press their noses against the windows as if they've never been out of the city before. Some of them get bus-sick because of the stuff they've eaten. And a couple of them only ever turn up to school when there's a camp coming on; and they get away with it.

Paul Kelly drove the school-bus. He was real smart the way he organised the Camp. His idea at a meeting before we left was that the students make up the rules on behaviour together and write them down. On the Camp it was harder to break rules that you helped work out – although three of our girls got into a brawl in the dunnies with some girls from another school.

"It wasn't our fault," they said to Paul Kelly. "They shouldn't've called Tracey a moll."

Coming home today, we pulled into a service station for petrol. Most of the kids were exhausted and couldn't even keep awake, but some of us got off to buy something to drink. About ten minutes after leaving there, the cops pulled us over. I noticed Billy next to me getting real tense. They talked quietly to Paul Kelly, who then asked Billy to get off the bus with his bag for a moment. They took some tools out of his bag. You should have seen Paul Kelly's face. He went red with anger and embarrassment.

It sure took the edge off the week. It was extra quiet all the rest of the way home, and kids kept throwing looks at Billy.

"I didn't pinch them," he kept saying to me with this

strange look in his eyes.

It was a dumb thing for him to keep saying, because we all saw them taken out of his bag. And no kidding, I wished I was sitting somewhere else. I felt embarrassed with him sitting next to me as my friend.

"I didn't pinch them. They were just lying there and I thought they had been thrown away," he finally said to me.

"How could it be worth it?" I felt like saying to him, but didn't. I had nothing to say to him for the rest of the way back.

Sunday April 19th

Back in January, Andy went crazy and dug a pond in the backyard. He chose a spot under an old plum tree, surrounded by young tree ferns, snails, slaters, and spiders. He sat watching the hose fill the pond, and sat watching it empty as the water soaked away through the soil. Then he put a layer of bricks, stones, and sand, on the floor, and sat watching the hose fill the pond, and sat watching it empty as the water soaked away through the soil. Then he got a large sheet of tin from a demolition site, and pounded and buckled it into the pond-floor terrain he liked. And as if he couldn't bear the sight of tin, once in position he covered it with the sand, rocks and stones. He sat watching the hose fill the pond, and sat watching it as it rose to the level he wanted, and stay there.

He then disappeared for most of the following Sunday on his bike, and returned in the afternoon with a jar of tadpoles, which he released into the pond. They rapidly all disappeared over the week, so he gathered another lot, and this time put a wire-mesh cover over their new home for protection. Over tea, we asked him why he wanted to keep tadpoles.

"I'm growin' frogs," he said like Dr. Frankenstein. "They

sound good and they'll protect our vegetables from insects."

He watched them day to day as they matured, and, to be honest, it got me too. Then unexpectedly they all disappeared. It didn't seem to worry Andy this time – he made no alterations to the pond which was building up a good slime.

"They're just hiding and turning into frogs," he said.

The days went past and then the weeks, and I was beginning to feel sorry for him because he was just about living out there watching over an empty pond. I tried talking him into emptying the pond and having a look to see what had happened, mainly because I felt sorry for him – you know, like it's better to tell a kid there's no Father Christmas. Anyway he wouldn't let me, so I finally locked him in the garage and then bailed all the water out of the pond. Nothing – only rocks, and sand, and slime. Andy got out of the garage and came running up. He looked down at my work. To complete the job, I pulled the sheet of tin out, and as rock and sand tumbled out, there amongst the debris about thirty premature frogs tried to jump about. Their lives had been turned into a national disaster. I tried to apologise to Andy because I felt like a lump of shit. He just looked at me as if I was some sort of psychopathic massmurderer and needed to be locked away. Two weeks later he released fifty geckos into the backyard, he said to do the same job, and this time, real formally in front of Alec and Jackie at the table, he asked me not to hurt them. As if I wanted to.

Monday April 20th

I had to see Whiles, the metalwork teacher, outside the Creative Arts staffroom at lunchtime just because I was ten minutes late for his class.

"Wheeler, you're a dickhead," he said. "I'd expect a lot

more from you. So nick off, and don't be late again."

That was fine, except I knew I was getting off lightly because I was Alec's son, and because I'm an Australian. He's made some kids clean up the whole metalwork room at the end of the day for a week. And he's real impatient with kids who can't express themselves very well.

If it had been Paul Kelly telling me off, he would have invited me into the staffroom and had this serious talk. So why are teachers so different? Some are real dags, others are pigs; some treat you like an equal, some like a lump of shit; some are strict, others are real weak and have no control over their classes; some seem real backward and would have trouble tying up their shoe-laces; some are real crazy – like Whiles, and others are dopey and in another world; some wear ties and suits; others look like they're dressed by the Salvation Army – like Alec; some are slobs with food stains all over their fronts and their flies left open; some breathe tobacco or garlic or beer all over you; some say hello to you even if you don't first; others are real snobs. And yet they're all teachers; they've all got that power over you, that makes them feel strong enough to go up to the toughest kids and tell them what to do – even though they'd hate to meet them on the street. It's that power that makes them real comedians, even though their jokes are sick. I've been hanging around teachers all my life it seems, and something inside me still makes me feel nervous waiting outside a staff-room door – like I'm different to them, and not as important.

Tuesday April 21st

I've got a real bad conscience about something that will take a long time to go away. I was playing cricket out in the street with some other kids tonight after school. Andy and a couple of young kids were hanging about wanting to play, but they're too young and would only spoil the game, especially when we only had about an hour's light. The stray dog was with them, watching on, and if the ball went near them, he would pick it up and run off with it. After a while it got annoying having all these breaks while we tried to get the ball back. Anyway one time he picked the ball up and started running around with it. I screamed at him: "Put it down."

But he thought it was a game and kept running close to me, but not letting go of it. All the little kids were laughing, so I threw the cricket-bat at him to give him a fright. The bat hit him in the side, and he dropped the ball, and slumped on the ground. He got up yelping before I could do anything, and hobbled inside. I felt real dumb in front of the other kids.

Uncle Liam yelled from his front-gate: "Is that how you treat your dog?"

What worries me is that I should have been able to miss if I just wanted to give him a fright.

Wednesday April 22nd

Billy was up to something after school today.

"Hey Mark, come with me; I wanna show you something," he said.

I followed him down to the other end of the school through the deserted corridors and yard.

"Come in here," he said, standing outside the Girls' dunnies in Alec's Area.

"What are ya?" I said to him.

But he was real excited about something.

"Come on, no one's about. Have a look on the mirror. I'll keep watch."

I knew he wouldn't let me go until I looked. I went in, and saw in huge writing in lipstick was written –
        'Lesley Anherbrat 4 Alec Wheeler'

"I tell you, this chick's real rapt in your dad," Billy said when I came out again.

It was beginning to get on my nerves.

"How did you notice it was there?" I asked annoyed.

He gave me that dumb smart-arse smile, and started walking away with his hands in his pockets.

"I just know these things."

Thursday April 23rd

When someone's got all their clothes on, you forget they've got a body altogether. It's just like they're a face and hair balanced on top of clothes or school uniforms. If Alec's got his jocks on, or Jackie her undies, their bodies always look a little rounder . . . shorter. But naked, they look long and stronger like animals. Their bodies really flow – know what I mean? I'm not saying we're nudists or anything like that in our family, but Alec and Jackie have always walked around the house naked if they wanted to. It's real strange at school though in the changing-rooms for PE. A lot of kids hide behind towels when they're getting changed, or have showers with their bathers on. And I've heard the girls do that a lot too. Jackie reckons when she was a teacher, that when she got changed with the girls at the Baths, they were embarrassed to see her naked. And they were all females. At our school, the boys' showers are all joined together, but they reckon the girls' ones are hidden away separately in cubicles. That's crazy. Jackie reckons it's sexism.

The time I really love to see Alec and Jackie naked is in the bush. When we go camping on the land, if it isn't hot, they just roll around naked in the dam's water or the mud, or go walking through the bush. From a distance there isn't much difference between their bodies. Jackie lopes like a tiger, whereas Alec takes his time and strolls about, like he was in the Garden of Eden. I don't mind swimming with nothing on, but I don't like to walk through the bush that way. It makes me feel unguarded against the snakes and march-flies and mossies and the idiots going past in their hotted-up Holdens shooting at the kangaroo sign. Andy would give his clothes to the snakes I reckon. I remember when he was small, Jackie used to have a lot of trouble getting him to put his clothes on, and sometimes he used to hide them or leave them in the street. And he used to hold onto his dick a lot. Alec used to say it was good to see him looking after it. Up the land, if it's warm enough, he just strolls off by himself exploring the old diggings; and when he gets into the water, he can lie around in it for hours, and never gets sick of it or cold.

Andy and me saw Jackie and Alec doing it in the bush once. I've got to say, it was pretty embarrassing. I mean I know how it's done and all that, and I have seen them naked, and heard moans coming from the bedroom; but standing there watching this funny looking struggle going on made me feel awkward – especially with Andy standing there next to me with wide eyes, gawking and smiling. I should have taken him away, but I wanted to see what happened too. When they had finished, they cuddled up, their faces looking real relaxed and happy, their eyes closed by the sun. It was also warm and shining on the backs of Andy and me too, and the bush was silent except for the birds and a slight breeze and the drone of a bush-fly; and suddenly I didn't feel embarrassed any more, and felt happy for them too. I thought, it is like they say, it feels good and there's nothing to be guilty about.

The only other time I have seen people have sex was these two kids on a camp last year. I watched through the hole of a tent with two other kids while the two randiest kids in the school tried to do it. This boy was always talking about sex. He reckons he first had sex when he was ten. And everyone said the girl was supposed to be a real nymphomaniac. Anyway Billy had arranged it so that we could watch. When I looked, he was lying on top of her, and even though she had her jeans and knickers pulled down, he still had his on. He seemed to be in a real hurry. Then he rolled over looking sort of guilty and seemed to want to get out of there, with this little wet patch showing on his pants. She looked silly with her pants down as if she hadn't started yet. I reckon she would have loved to have done it the way Alec and Jackie did in the bush.

At times I really wouldn't mind having sex myself; just to see what it feels like. But who would I have it with? That's the scary part. I mean how do you go about asking someone if they want to have sex with you? The whole thing's just too scary. But wanting to see naked bodies is something different altogether. If I see girls wearing bathers, all of a sudden I start trying to imagine how they'd look naked. It's not that I want to do anything necessarily; it's just something inside of me gets my brain working.

Tuesday April 28th

This little kid was knocked over on the crossing outside the school today. There were hundreds of kids standing around watching and teachers running around not knowing what to do; and I suppose everyone was waiting for the ambulance. There was a lot of blood on the road and he was stone white. Someone had put a blanket over his chest and legs, and there was a little girl holding onto his hand and screaming. And there was a guy with a bakery uniform on who was running around doing nothing, and he was pale too and his eyes were looking everywhere, and all he seemed to want to do was run in one direction and never stop. And he kept on saying to one of the teachers that the little kid just ran out without looking; and sometimes he would go and put his head on the door of his van where the window was open; it was as if that was the only thing that could hold him up. I went away thinking that one family's life had all of a sudden been changed.

Wednesday April 29th

There's a picture in the photo-album of Jackie sitting around on a motor-bike with about four other friends also on bikes. They all have white tee-shirts on with scraggy old leather jackets and worn jeans. They all look bored as if their faces are made of leather too. Jackie had short hair and looked pretty tough, although it's hard to see her face because she's looking at the ground.

"Did you like being a bikie?" I asked her once.

She smiled: "I wasn't really a bikie, but I loved being on my bike – especially out on the highway."

"Why?"

"Because you're not enclosed. You're open to the wind and the smells and the rain; and it's all around you and all over you," she said, holding onto the arms of the chair as if she was going to do a wheelie.

"Why haven't you still got a bike?" chipped in Andy.

She looked thoughtful, as if she liked being asked the question: "I guess I don't like the noise they make any more."

"Was Alec ever a bikie?" I asked.

She laughed this time.

"No. He was too straight. I couldn't even get him on the back," she said.

Thursday April 30th

You know I reckon most of the Australian kids at school only have one parent. That always seems to be the story, like today when the teacher was gathering information about our parents and their occupations from us. They usually have big families and a whole lot of hangers-on which makes it even harder. Makes me feel sort of safe and luckier than them, as if they would swap with me given the chance any time. Alec raves on for hours about this.

"I just can't understand how some kids can be so ill-treated and still surface at the age of thirteen or fourteen, sane, warm and sensitive," he says often.

Sunday May 3rd

This is amazing weather. It's still like summer and it'll be winter soon. Alec reckons that the summers in Melbourne seem to be arriving later and lasting longer as the years pass. Both of us were sitting out in the garden late this afternoon. He was preparing some school work for tomorrow and I was fiddling with my guitar. He even let me have a glass of beer. You know there are times when he's not like my father, but my best friend. We both had our shirts off and were just sitting there in bare feet and jeans, and I had this feeling that even though I knew him, there were still millions of things to discover about him. And he got up and did his usual thing of wandering through the vegetables and checking the new growth on the trees; and even though the light was fading, his body looked just great, as if he was Tarzan of the vegetables and I was his chimp watching on. I just feel he's always there and always will be when needed. It was good to see him smiling to himself too and wanting to chat with me all the time because over the past few weeks his mind has been a million miles away concerned about something else.

Sunday May 10th

Stray dogs can disappear as suddenly as they arrive. The

stray's been gone about a week now. At first we were sure he was straying out for a few nights, but I reckon he'll never come home now. He's only been with us for two months, but he really fitted in and was just a great dog. No one else is saying much, but I get the feeling we've all got our eye out for him just about all the time. Even the neighbours said they'd watch out for him. Alec drove Andy and me all around the streets, but there was no sign of him. Alec reckons he might have been exploring when suddenly he picked up a scent he knew, which might have been his real home, and off he went. Andy reckons he could have got hit by a car. Anyway he wasn't at the Dog's Home either. I just hope he's okay. I still keep thinking of when I threw the bat at him.

Wednesday May 27th

You'd think Alec could give school a rest. We've just had the May holidays, and here he was again tonight at tea bloody boring everyone about some kid who has been going crazy all the time, and has run out of chances. That's all he does, talk about kids who frustrate him because he can't help them. This kid sounded real violent.

"We were in the Vice-Principal's office," Alec said. "We had Kevin there and his parents. There we were sitting there like bloody judges telling them that Kevin wasn't going to get another chance. It seems his mother is just out of hospital. You should have seen her fight for her son's survival." He laughed and sort of sneered at the same time. "At one stage she straight out begged and pleaded, like it was all she had left." He laughed that same way again. "The whole thing was crazy. The law states that he has the right to an education until the age of fifteen."

"He's also one of the reasons why you're having hot flushes and headaches, Alec," Jackie said. "And why you bloody mumble in your sleep all night."

Alec didn't even seem to listen to that. He went on: "His step-father, this worn-out looking guy, didn't say a word the whole time. He just looked at the floor and his hands all the time. He's taken on a family of five, three in their early and mid-teens. He's on worker's comp. with a crushed arm."

Alec stopped and looked confused: "It turned out that Kevin's first father used to beat hell out of him and made him sleep under the bed or in a tool-shed. And do you know what she said at the end? She said Kevin was the only one who brought her a cup of tea in bed when she got out of hospital."

Thursday May 28th

"How come you fell for him?" I asked Jackie.

She thought for a moment.

"He was different," she said.

"You met him at University, right?" I prodded on.

"Right. What are you up to?" she smiled. "I'd seen him around for about a year and only spoken to him twice. Then one night there was a Ball, we had a dance and that was that."

I sat back and slurped on my cup of tea. Then I realised she hadn't answered my question.

"What do you mean, he was different?"

"I guess he was different because he wasn't trying to be different," she answered. "I was going through some pretty crazy times, but when I was with him I felt I could be just me. Anyway I liked his mixture. He seemed relaxed and kind and moped around like a dag – and was a little unattainable."

"Unattainable?" I asked.

"Yes, you know, when you're uncertain whether you can get what you want and so that only makes you want it more," she said, giving me an English lesson.

"You wanted to marry him?"

She laughed: "No. We were only living together when Andy was born."

"You wanted to have sex with him?" slipped out.

"No," she laughed again. "I wanted him to love me."

We were silent for a while, as if she was waiting for my next question.

"Some of the kids at school go together," I said, getting closer to what I wanted to talk about.

Jackie opened her eyes wide.

"And why do you think they go together?" she asked.

That was something I had thought about a lot. Funny, I was trying to answer for them – not for myself.

"It sort of looks good to be going with someone, especially if that person is good-looking or hard to get."

"And are they the only reasons?" she wanted to know.

"I reckon both of them usually want to have sex . . . Anyway that's what they try and show everybody else."

"And do they have sex?" she asked.

"Nah, I bet they don't," I sorta sniggered. "They're too scared."

"Of what?" Now she was asking all the questions.

"Of their parents, I reckon. And of asking each other to do it," I said. "When you were fourteen, did you want to have sex?"

"Sometimes." She looked straight at me. "There were times I felt so strongly about it, that I was just about ready to rape the first guy who came along. But I was too afraid of my parents and wasn't sure how to do it."

We fell silent again and finished our mugs of tea.

"Anyway," I said. "They don't usually go together for very long because they're so scared of being dropped by the other that they get in first and drop the other person." I thought a minute. "I guess it's hard to get love when you're my age."

I felt sure once I had used the word 'love' that she would

ask me what the word meant to me. But she didn't.

"Would you like to be in love with someone at school?" she asked instead.

"No way," I lied. "There are too many problems involved."

"Would you like girls to love you?" she said.

"If they want to." I sounded real generous. "Anyway how can you tell if someone's rapt in you?"

I had tried to sound pretty bored, but this was the information I had been after all the time.

Jackie thought a moment: "Perhaps she'll look at you longer than she should."

That's what Cathy Roussos did, but only for two weeks. I started running through all the girls who I wanted to look at me longer than they should. That only made me feel real disappointed.

Friday May 29th

I keep remembering something Alec said over the May holidays.

"This house is becoming a burden," I heard him say out aloud to himself. "A real burden."

I could kind of see his frustration, but didn't understand what he wanted from the house. We haven't even lived in it for a year yet, and for just that time it has been continued hard work reblocking, plastering, painting, sanding floors, rewiring, building a sunroom, turning a rubbish-tip into a garden of fruit, trees, and vegetables; stripping paint off doors, sand-papering, pipe-laying, replacing glass, noise; missing out on holidays; trying to save money; bruises, splinters, cuts, bandaids, antiseptic; enormous bins carting away all the rubbish in the early morning; trying to get dust out of our ears, our eyes, and noses, from beneath our fingernails, from our backs, necks and hair, and out of the food.

Hard work, but I thought we had all been happy with it. After all, we had learnt to be trades-people together. Of course, Alec has done a lot more than the rest of us, but he is stronger. None of us can keep on as long, and the dust has played hell with Andy's asthma. But there is something else about Alec. It's like he's addicted to the work – he skips meals, is up to about 3:00am in the morning finishing off jobs, gets moody a lot if he isn't working, as if he feels guilty about it.

And it's been impossible to try and get him to leave it for a while. He just smiles at you, ruffles your hair or wrestles, then climbs up a ladder and starts stripping paint off the roof. Jackie doesn't seem to think there is such a rush; I reckon she would be happy to live anywhere, and I can't see the rush either. In fact I kind of liked the way the house was when we moved in, even though the plaster was falling off the walls and the roof leaked. We used to light roaring fires in the huge old fireplace and sit around it in the dark telling stories, and eating fantastic meals which were on the floor in old cast-iron pots. And you didn't have to look after everything and watch things you did, because everything was already grubby and dirty.

But Alec is teaching as well as doing all this, and sometimes you can see a little battle going on between what he should do at night, work on the house, or work for school. Alec and Jackie's biggest worry is money. They got loans from all over the place to buy the house, and this fixing it up is costing a load. Alec says it's better to find the money now, because in the future everything will cost so much more.

"Why is it a burden?" I said surprising him.

"Oh, I don't know. All the work we've done has come undone, the walls are all cracked again, we need new plaster-board. The damp has returned, the house needs painting on the outside, there is still the verandah to do – and we have no money, mate," he said, grinning.

"Who cares about those things?" I said. "It's fine how it is."

He gave that same smile.

"It's got to be finished so it can be forgotten about. And other things can be done."

"Well, what do you call finished?" I asked.

He shrugged his shoulders: "I suppose when your family has a warm comfortable house to live in that other people enjoy coming to. A place where you don't have to worry about anything for a long time."

"You mean 'you and your family' don't you?" butted in Jackie, who had walked in and overheard the last bit.

"That's right," he said. "All of us."

Monday June 1st

There's this mad little Egyptian kid, Joe, at school who climbs up on the lockers, and jumps on anyone who goes past. He's always telling lies to the teachers. He's cross-eyed and wears a leather jacket right through summer and winter. I couldn't believe it; Paul Kelly walked past and he tried to jump on his neck, but missed, and landed on his side.

"Sir . . . Sir," he screamed, "I've broken my wrist."

Paul Kelly didn't believe him.

"Good," he said. "You deserve it." And he walked on.

But Joe kept yelling, so me and Charlie took him down to the PE Office because PE teachers are like doctors. Our PE teacher is this big American guy who reckons the school is really slack, and keeps talking about how strict it is out in the mid-West, wherever that is.

"Give us a look, son," he said to Joe, with his slow lazy accent.

Anyway it turned out that his wrist was broken in two places and he had to be taken to hospital. But before he was taken, he kept blubbering that Mr Kelly said it was good

67

that he had broken his wrist. I mean he just wouldn't let up. And the PE teacher looked real angry about it.

"It just shows you how much they care with their slack beliefs," he sort of said to himself and Charlie and me at the same time.

It's crazy how things can get so easily confused.

Tuesday June 2nd

We were in the lounge tonight. Andy had gone to bed, and Jackie was just sitting there staring angrily at Alec.

"So when are we allowed a little more of your time?" she said sarcastically.

"What do you mean?" he answered yawning, looking stuffed, and trying a weak smile.

"Oh come off it, Alec," she said. "I mean you have a family at home also. I mean you haven't been home before 6:00pm for weeks. I mean you are either at a meeting or visiting parents, or trying to organise some amazing new programme for your other family."

He went quiet for a moment.

"The kids leave school and have nowhere to go," he said. "There's no stigma attached any more to returning to the family for support. They're lucky if they end up factory fodder. There's hours of planning that have to go into setting up the teaching of the right survival skills for them –"

"Jesus Christ," she said, butting in. "All we get are the left-overs; the exhausted ghost that rolls in every night."

He looked disappointed. "I would hope you would think more freely than that," he said.

"Who's trying to take your goddam freedom away?" she said. "But things changed when we had our two blue-eyed babies; when you insisted on buying a house when we were broke; when you decided to become super-teacher on your home ground."

"What would you prefer? Hide away?" he said nastily.

To be honest, I didn't have a clue about what they were talking about except I agree with Jackie that we only get to see him when he's real tired.

Saturday June 6th

You know there's one thing really weird about our place. There's spiders everywhere. You should have seen them in summer, but even now just getting into winter, I could show you a lot. They reckon spiders disappear in the cold weather, but not these. They're around the sheds and they've built thick black homes beneath the eaves of the roof and the surrounds of the outside windows. And if you go out at night with a torch and shine it up into the Cypress tree you'll see big ones, that's for sure. We all say you should pay respect towards them because they eat flies and other pests that get into the garden, but I reckon we all get the creeps from them a little, they're so hairy and silent. Sometimes if they're big enough, they'll make a tiny soft padding noise as they cross a wall or rustle a paper or make a glass ring a little. The only time I kill them is when they come inside the house, and they're those big huntsmen that sit in the corner on the ceiling of your bedroom, waiting for the chance to drop down on your face in the dark and paralyse you and sew your eyelids together with their threads and slowly suck the insides of your body out through your mouth and nose, feeding on you alive for weeks and weeks.

Andy said he might have seen the stray yesterday. It was a long way away and chasing some other kid on a bike.

Tuesday June 9th

I guess what I discovered was really an accident. Normally

I wouldn't have looked through Alec's school things because, let's face it, who would want to look at a pile of other kids' work? But this folder was pushed into a side-pocket of his school-bag as if it was top secret or something. His bag which he had left sitting in front of me on the table before he went outside had fallen slightly open, and the manilla-folder was just asking to be taken out.

It contained a lot of poetry and pieces of Creative Writing that had been marked but not given back. I read a couple which seemed pretty good, and then I was attracted by a page that had been folded over. It had 'For Alec' printed neatly on the outside. I opened it and it read:

> "Alec, I love your eyes, your hair, your lips, your moods and mannerisms, everything that is you. I can't help it Alec, I love you and want you."
> *Lesley A.*

I could feel the anger building up inside me before I had even finished reading it. My face went hot and my mind kept repeating that it was a joke, a piece of kid's stuff. Some kid making fun of my dad. What right did she have to write something like that to him? It wasn't funny.

And then there was Alec coming in the back-door, and me hurrying to get the folder back in his bag. He looked at me bewildered as if he couldn't understand why I wasn't answering him.

I can't write any more tonight. My imagination is going crazy. Why didn't he throw it away? Why is it still in his bag? He must be going to show it to her and tell her to stop being stupid.

Wednesday June 10th

I sure did get excited about that letter yesterday; all for nothing, I reckon. I mean girls get crushes on teachers all the time, and boys do too. At first the words in her dumb letter kept screaming out in my brain and repeating themselves over and over again. In a way, I guess I might have been a bit jealous, because I didn't want anyone else liking my dad like that. I suppose really I should feel sorry for her. Alec might be like a father for her. But I still can't help thinking how beautiful and older-looking she is; and those dumb things Andy said, and what I saw in the Girls' dunnies. I would like to talk to Alec about it; usually we can talk about anything, but it would look like I've been snooping and that I might believe crazy things. And I reckon I don't have the right to go around judging people just because of my own imagination or jealousy. I'd just like it cleared up, you know, so that I never think about it.

If only this Lesley could have been in the loungeroom tonight. Alec was sitting watching a film with Jackie between his arms and legs, and he was caressing her head. She would have seen what a dumb thing it was to write that letter.

Funny what I did yesterday, when Alec was standing there looking bewildered at me. I got up, my face burning, went past him and out into the yard where it was a bit chilly, and decided to climb up the Cypress tree and be alone for a while. Only about a third of the growth on the tree is green. All the rest is dead, making it look like it has grey hair. Its lower trunk is completely bared of foliage now, and the wrinkly grey bark makes the tree sort of crippled and buckled looking. I climbed it slowly, careful of the sharp edges of its bark, and my mind on the giant huntsmen that slept somewhere within it during the day. At first it was easy because where the lower trunk divided, it was a good height to swing into and balance on, but as I tried to climb higher I realised its lack of lower new branch growth meant there was nothing to hang onto. I started to wonder how Andy could get to the top. To continue I would have to hands and heels it, which wouldn't be much fun on that bark. Then I saw a spot which was an intersection between one of the main forks and an out-hanging branch. I climbed onto the branch and found by sitting on it with my back against the fork, it was like being in an arm-chair.

A sun's ray fell directly on my face, and when I closed my eyes, I felt the earth rocking gently below me. And I felt far more relaxed, and way above any crazy thoughts.

Thursday June 11th

You can always tell if a teacher's got a hang-over. They walk real careful into the first class of the day, and they look pale and dark around the eyes as if they've just got up, and they are carrying a glass of water, and they're not in a good mood and don't want to talk and they set you work from a book to go on with, and they look like they can hardly wait until the end of the day, and the class is real boring, and we usually try and keep a bit quieter, but if it's Paul Kelly we wait our chance and go and scream in his ear.

Saturday June 13th

Guess what. I had to have five stitches just above my ear. The doctor at the clinic reckons I might have a headache for a while, but it seems to be going already. It's real strange when they start sticking needles into your head. Must be hard to find somewhere to stick it without it going through your brain. It was a box of matches' fault. I had just lit a fire in the lounge last night and I threw the matches up in the air and marked them, and that was that, a re-enactment of the 1977 Grand Final was on, and I was zigzagging all around the house, and kicking goals from nowhere, and taking spectacular marks, and I avoided five Collingwood players in the hallway and kicked this phenomenal goal from an impossible angle through my open bedroom doorway, and

I went down from a charge from behind knocking the door closed, and as I was picking myself up from the ground with the matches under my arm, Andy charged into the bedroom to get something and the door-knob went right into my ear and through my brain.

So the game was called off, and Andy kept saying: "What's wrong?"

Jackie drove me to the clinic, and they had to shave a patch of hair away where they stitched, and for sure when I get to school on Monday morning everyone's going to want to know whether I was in a fight, and I'll string them along and make up about four different stories of what happened.

Sunday June 14th

The telephone rang just before tea, and Andy and me had a race to get it. He got there first because he had an unfair start. He stood there like a dumb blob, spluttering repeatedly into the receiver: "Hello . . . Hello . . . Hello . . . No one's there," he said, hanging up. "I bet I know who that was."

"Who?" I said.

"Never mind, it's a secret," he said, and ran into the bedroom and locked the door from the inside before I could catch him.

Would you believe it but an hour later the phone went again. When I picked it up and said hello, someone hung up straight away. I looked around, and Andy was standing in the doorway smirking stupidly. I knew what he was thinking, and it was no joke any more. I decided right then I was going to talk to this girl at school tomorrow.

Monday June 15th

I sort of sneaked around Alec's Area and the canteen before

school and during recess and lunch, but didn't see her. Real casual like, I asked this kid I know in the Area whether he had seen her.

"She's not at school," he said. "She only comes when she wants to. She's a real moll they reckon. She's rapt in your father, you know."

I looked up the telephone directory and got her address from there.

So after school I went to visit Lesley Anherbrat. It really freaked me. I guess I'm still shaking a bit. I had decided I was going to ask her about what I saw in the Girls' dunnies, and being real sneaky like a detective, try and let her spill the information I wanted by talking too much.

Her house was in one of those small streets surrounded by high-rise flats and factories and hotels and railway bridges. The street was full of tiny little weatherboard houses with picketed fences that sided onto each other and you'd reckon in a strong wind they'd fall over like a pack of cards. I must have hung around on the corner for about fifteen minutes getting up enough courage to act.

She answered the door herself. At first she squinted as if trying to remember someone from school. I could see her brain working through her eyes.

"Do you remember me at the party?" I said. "I go to your school too. I'm Mark Wheeler. Alec Wheeler is my dad."

She looked real surprised. I reckon she was just putting me together from the party when some guy appeared from behind her. He stood in the half shadow of the hallway, but even in that light straight away I felt I was looking at some gangster from an old movie. He had a shadow of stubble on his face; his hair was short and curly and greasy, and he only had a tee-shirt on, in winter, and loose pants. He stood behind her, and one tattooed arm rested on her shoulder.

"So what do you want?" he said with this soft controlled voice. I was being treated like some door-to-door salesman. Her eyes caught mine and there was a message all over them.

Don't say anything.

"Mark's a friend of mine from school, Ron," she said. "He's going to help me with some work."

He looked straight into my eyes. I reckon this guy was dangerous; his silence really freaked me. He stepped back and Lesley stood back beside him.

"Come in, then," he said in that soft voice.

There was no way I wanted to go in. I could feel my ears burning as I walked past them inside. The house smelled as if the windows were never opened. It had a minimum of furniture in it as if people came and went all the time.

"Want some coffee?" she asked, leading me into the loungeroom.

I sat in a huge chair. Ron stood at the doorway and pulled out a mangled cigarette from his back pocket. I tried hard not to watch her leave the room, but I couldn't help staring at the purple on one of her cheeks and under her chin that she had tried to hide with heavy make-up. Were they bruises? They sure looked like it. Did this guy bash her? He gave her the once over also as she left the room.

"Nice arse, eh?" he asked me, lighting the cigarette.

I couldn't believe it. I was a prisoner, for sure. Nowhere to look, and him standing at the door.

"Quiet boy . . . and in the wrong neighbourhood," he said softly. "I'm Lesley's uncle. I look after her and make sure she doesn't get into any mischief. She's only fifteen, but she's been a woman for three years."

I sat there real dumb, looking at the TV set that was turned off.

"So what work are you helping her with?" he said, staring at me.

I could feel my cheeks burning. It was as if I was about to have a fight and couldn't get out of it. Then I started to feel hate, real hate for this guy.

"Cat got your tongue?" he said, and the tone of his voice never changed. "You know what I'd do, son? I'd get the hell out of here."

I stood up like a robot and walked slowly out of the house. As I passed him in the doorway, I could sense his lips quivering. Around the corner, I felt the sweat between my legs and under my arms. That guy had to be an escaped convict.

Thursday June 25th

Somebody went and dug up and stole half the saplings and other small plants from the front garden. It really made everyone feel disappointed because we'd been watching them grow for nearly a year, really looking after them. I wonder when they were taken. Usually someone's at home. It gives you the creeps – it's the same as if someone had been walking around your room after breaking in. I don't reckon any plant lovers would have done it. Who would do a thing like that? I tell you, this suburb is full of thieves and violent people; nothing like where we used to live.

Sunday July 5th

That drink really fooled me. It had given and taken away at the same time. What it had given me was this real strong feeling that I could do anything – and that's why I decided to walk home, which is about five kilometres from Skating. I can't even remember making the decision to walk. I just remember marching along like some sort of soldier who was having trouble stopping himself from flying. I was swinging my arms back and forwards and seemed to have forgotten all about police divi-vans and muggers and crazy alsatians and that you had to stop on corners for red lights and that the last tram had probably just gone past. In fact time and distance didn't seem to exist. But what the drink took from me was the energy to keep it up. With only about one kilometre to go, my legs went like lead, my heart was thudding, and I was so dry I could hardly swallow. By the time I turned into the top of our street, I remember that I was mumbling to myself about having to get home.

And boy, was my brain working overtime. No arguments . . . just quiet, I thought to myself. And twice now Alec has stayed over at friends' places on weekends, to work. I must talk to her at school. I was too scared that day. Didn't have a chance. And he's never seemed so far away. Just a lot of crazy thoughts swimming around.

From then on it took a lot of effort and concentration to push leg after leg forward to make it, and even then, with one house to go, I nearly decided to lie down on the footpath and have a rest. To be honest, I've never been pissed before, and looking back to last night, I'm glad some neighbour didn't find me struggling around on the concrete like some fish out of water.

It's normal to leave the roller-skating place sometimes to go outside and hang around. Some kids leave their skates on and have a Coke or a cigarette or just talk sitting on bonnets of cars. Billy and this kid Nick said we should go out and have a drink, and Billy looked at me as if it was some sort of challenge. Outside he said we should go around the corner to the old mill where his older brother sometimes hung out. There was a group of about six other kids, sitting and talking around two cars. They were drinking beer out of a bottle and some vermouth and port, which they passed around in the circle. At first we were ignored as small fish, but Billy made sure we were included. Maybe I joined in because I was looked at as some sort of goodie-goodie, maybe I was too weak to say no, I don't know. I sure began to talk a lot though, after a while, and laugh and crack jokes – and I never do that in a group. They kept telling me to shut up, and one big kid kept shoving me, but I didn't care.

There was a light on in the lounge. I remember deciding

to sneak in the back way and go straight to bed. In the side-way I suddenly felt giddy and I fell into the bamboo-bush. I must have scratched all my arms, but I didn't feel a thing. I got to my feet again and got a real scare from this feeling that I was turning upside down. My feet spread by themselves and my hands started looking around for something to hold on to, and I suppose it was then that I realised I was drunk. I lurched forward and found the Cypress which I clung on to. There was no warmth in the trunk and the bark was rough. The next moment I was down on my hands and knees as if I was waiting for something. And then I went really giddy and felt real sick. I dry-retched first, and then the spew came, twice. I was too scared to move even. I spewed a third time and that's when I felt a hand on my back. It was Jackie rubbing gently in a circular motion.

"That's right," she said. "Get it all out."

It's funny but right then I felt a little better. She helped me take some deep breaths. I felt worn out and scared to move, but my head was clearing. I remember apologising all the time. She didn't say anything, but the hand stopped circling my back and slipped beneath my side. I felt her face rest on the back of my neck.

"Is Alec home?" I gulped.

"No," she said, sounding a long way away. "He's gone off on a school camp."

I tell you. I didn't feel too hot this morning. Andy doesn't even know, and I guess I won't tell him. It wasn't until today that I started wondering about Alec being on this camp. Usually he talks about them a lot during the previous week, and I've never known him to leave on a weekend. And there's this feeling I've got about our place at the moment. I don't know how to put it. . . . . It's like it's growing empty.

Monday July 6th

It poured all day today. It was so heavy we had to get some

saucepans out and put them on the floor where it was dripping in three places through the ceiling.

"Hope they've got good tents on the camp," Andy said to Jackie during tea. "Otherwise Dad'll get real drenched."

She didn't answer him, just reached across and squeezed his hand. We've always been able to talk of just about anything in our family. And right now there are some things I'm just busting to ask about. But it's the way Jackie's behaving, as if she's hiding her true feelings; and it's like without saying anything she's asking that I don't say or ask anything. Does that make sense?

I got Andy to talk about his dream over tea too. This morning when the alarm went off, I rolled over and there he was lying on his back staring at the ceiling, like he'd had no sleep all night.

"You okay?" I said.

He started to breathe heavily and his eyes went all watery. "Just a bad dream," he mumbled.

So he told us all about it tonight, and no kidding I reckon it did him good because I've never heard him talk so long uninterrupted. It turns out he was Dracula's servant and always being watched by these piercing blood-red eyes. Each time he tried to escape, he got lost and was caught and hurt by Dracula for it. Anyway Dracula's wife tried to help him escape once. When Dracula found out, he went real bananas, and started to peel her skin off like strips of bark, and he made Andy help him, and that's when he woke up.

"Yuk," said Jackie. "No more TV for you."

But he looked at her real serious.

"And you were Dracula's wife," he said quietly. "And that's when I got real frightened. . . ."

"And he wet the bed," I told her.

Tuesday July 7th

I didn't know it was Billy's birthday today until he showed

79

me this really old watch.

"It was my mother's grandfather's," he said, taking it in and out of his pocket about eight times on its fading silver chain. "She reckons she's been saving it for me for when I turned fifteen because she wanted me to have it especially."

I sure wished I had it.

"Happy Birthday," I said, and I couldn't get over just how proud he was; like it was the greatest event of his life. You should have seen his face.

And would you believe it but he had just put it away at lunchtime after showing me it again in the dunnies, when in barged three older kids, and just for fun, pushed us both against the wash-basins.

"Watch my watch," Billy started to scream, but they didn't know what he meant. He must have felt it crushed in his pocket because he went berserk.

"I'm going to kill you, you bleeding pooftas," he said, rushing at them. "My brother will kill you!"

One of them hit him in the face to stop him. "Take it easy. It was only an accident," this kid said, and the three of them pissed off.

He chased them a bit, then came back and stood at the mirrors, taking broken glass out of his pocket and putting bits on the wash-basin.

"I'm going to kill them," he said, and he was trying to wipe the tears off his face. "I'm going to kill them. I'm going to shoot them with my dad's gun."

It was real pathetic to look at him in the mirror. He was trying to sniff blood up his nose again; he'd wiped some of it across his cheek and chin, and the bits of the watch were in front of him.

"Me mum told me not to bring it to school," he said. "She said something would happen to it. I told her I wanted to show you because you were my best mate."

And all the time, he was handling the pieces, trying to work out if they could go back together.

"I'm going to kill them," he said.

Billy's always trying; but he hardly ever wins.

Thursday July 9th

Jesus, what's going on? Two cops were at the door just now, and they wanted to know if Alec was home. I didn't say anything. I just went and got Jackie, and she looked real worried and told me to go down to the shop and pick up the milk. I asked her if everything was okay, and she said not to worry and she would tell me later. At the front-gate I still managed to hear one of the policemen say that they were looking for the whereabouts of Lesley Anherbrat. And that's all Jackie told me when I got home too.

"Some girl in Alec's Area at school has sneaked off from home," she said.

I wonder if she's on the camp.

Friday July 10th

I like sitting next to Charlie; we can both do things our own way, without copying off each other. But if I'm next to Billy, he always mucks around and at the last moment wants to copy down what I've done. He reckons just because we've been talking, then somehow the writing I do belongs to the both of us. And although he's never said it, he expects friends to always cover for each other. I would be doing that all the time though, because although he's good in class discussions, he can barely read or write properly. We had this memory test in Maths today, and at the last moment I sat on the other side of the room from him. I don't reckon he could answer one question. He was really spitting chips at Recess and looking to fight me or hurt me somehow.

"'Your father's a poofta,'" he sneered at me.

"Why?" I said, wondering what the dick-head meant.

"He thinks he's a big shot around the place," he answered.

I could see in his eyes he was desperate for something to say next. Charlie started dragging me away to the canteen and seemed to think it was all pretty funny.

"And you're both chickens," he yelled after us.

Sometimes it's pretty hard to like Billy. He always expects so much of me; and he's always trying to butt in on my friendship with Charlie.

Andy brought this kid home after school. His name is Colin and he stutters all the time. Andy explained spitting all over us that Colin stutters a lot because when he was small an alsatian jumped up on him and bit him on the cheek and since then he stutters. He is one of those kids who has red hair and freckles, and looks like he should never go out into the sun. I reckon it's about the first time Andy has ever brought anyone home from school. He seemed rapt.

He showed Colin around and then they went out in the backyard with two huge banana and peanut-butter sandwiches each that Andy had made. They started this game where they would run at each other and just before colliding, both would spin away and faint into the grass. No kidding, they must have played it for about an hour. Anyway they finally got exhausted I suppose, because they came in and Andy made two more of those sandwiches, and Colin stayed for tea and during it pulled a little car out of his pocket and played with it on the table, pushing it around the plates and salt and pepper shakers and the bread-board.

I said to Jackie I thought Alec would have been home by now today. She said he wasn't expected till early next week.

Saturday July 11th

The telephone went just after lunch and before I left for the footy. Jackie and me got to it at the same time. She picked it up and I don't know why but I sort of stood watching her wondering who it was. As she listened, she started to go real pale and stare hard at me.

She said: "I don't believe you," but kept listening and then said: "No, he's not."

Her eyes started to go real watery, and her lips sort of fell apart a little and a bubble of slag seemed to be trying to push out.

Finally she got real angry and started to scream: "You just watch your threats, buddy-boy . . ."

And she slammed the phone down and looked right through me as if I was a ghost. She picked up her coat and ran out the front door. I'm not sure, but I think she didn't want me to see her cry. I ran out the front to see what I could do.

"Leave me alone," she said. "Don't worry; sex maniacs really upset me."

So I walked around the house for a while trying to clean things up to help that way. I didn't go to the footy. I hung around until she came home and it turned out to be a real quiet afternoon. I sure wished Alec had been home today to talk to her.

Sunday July 12th

Some older kids are going crazy I reckon – especially in our street. They really give me the shits. I mean everyone would love to have a car, but these guys are maniacs. They go up and down our street at a hundred miles an hour, and every time they go past our house, it's like a bomb has gone off and the whole house shakes. And they like to slam their brakes on, and then drag off throwing smoke and stones everywhere. And when we're playing footy or cricket on the road, we've learnt to scatter quick because there's no way they're going to stop for you and no kidding, one day they're going to splatter someone all over the street.

They seem to have this heavy sort of love affair with their cars. Sometimes you can see them just sit in their cars for hours, parked, staring out of the windscreens. Or they lie back and listen to their cassette tapes that fill the whole street with music. It's like they're living in their cars.

And the older girls sit out on their brick front fences and talk to them and sometimes if they're real lucky they get to sit in the car for a while. Those girls must be the dumbest things on this planet, the way they reckon these guys are just so fantastic. It's as if they owned the neighbourhood. No one ever goes out and tells them to be more careful or piss off. Everyone just stares out of their windows in amazement as the cars go past, waiting for the day when one drives right into their front bedroom.

If two of them pass each other, they slam on their brakes and hang out their windows talking about their cars and giving each other's cars the once over. And they do that until the traffic banks up behind them, and then they drag off. Just wait until I get my licence. I'm going to buy a tank and blast them off the road and make it safe for kids to play footy and cricket again. And I'll blast the girls too for being so dumb.

Monday July 13th

When Andy got up this morning to feed the chooks, he found them all dead. He called Jackie and me. It sure looked like a massacre. They were lying around inside the pen or just around the doorway, patches of dried blood over their bodies; and feathers everywhere. The wire on the hatch-door had been pushed in, and their perch and water and food and laying boxes were scattered everywhere amongst the straw like a chase had gone on. Andy didn't say any-thing. He just went and got a spade and started digging a hole underneath the fig-trees. I took the spade and did some digging for him. He walked around picking up his dead chooks and chucking them into the hole. Then he went inside and had his breakfast.

"Dogs," said Jackie, putting the things in the hatch back in place. "Once the chooks get them excited, they've got no chance, the poor buggers."

The Greek guy next door said he wouldn't think twice about shooting dogs to protect his chooks or property.

Tuesday July 14th

The first thing I saw when I got to school this morning was the school mini-bus parked outside. Alec must be back from the camp, I figured, so I went to his Area to see him. Two girls I recognised from the party rushed up to me.

"Is your dad coming in today?" one said, looking pretty concerned.

"Isn't he here?" I asked.

"No," they said, looking at each other. "Is he all right?"

"What do you mean?" I wanted to know.

That's when they started to look embarrassed, and they began to glance all around like they didn't know what to say.

"What's going on?" I said, beginning to feel frightened. "When did you get back?"

"Last night," they said, still looking confused. "Haven't you heard? Your dad came back Sunday." And they hurried off to talk to a group of girls standing close by, like they had some important information for them.

So where was he? I decided to ring home, and see if he had arrived. No kidding, I could feel different kids staring at me as if I had become some sort of freak-show. No one answered the phone, and I had to get to class. Then Billy found me. He was nearly falling over with excitement.

"What did ya father say?" he asked me, his eyes flashing.

"What about?" I said, feeling more and more tense.

"The camp of course, and the guy."

"What guy?" I said.

"Stop acting smart; the guy on the camp." And suddenly he stopped looking excited, and stared at me. "Don't you know? All the kids are talking about it this morning."

And so he told me what he heard, about this tough guy turning up at the camp on Sunday and threatening everyone, and saying he was Lesley Anherbrat's uncle; and about how Alec had taken this other teacher's car and driven off with her.

"All the kids reckon your dad was saving her," he said.

"Oh, that," I said trying to think quickly and not panic. "I'm going for a piss."

I turned two corners, changed directions, and sprinted all the way home.

When I got there, Jackie was running around ready to go out. Andy sat quietly on the couch and for a change his hair was done. He looked worried.

"Quick Mark, if you want to come with us we're leaving now." And then she said right out of the blue: "We're going to see Alec. He's in hospital, he's had an accident."

She was trying to be calm, but the hand that held a cigarette was shaking.

"Is he okay?" I said, scared by how tense she was behaving.

"Yes."

In the car, I asked her when it happened.

"Last night, I think they said," she answered.

So I told her what they were saying at school, how Alec had rescued that girl. She didn't say anything, and her face remained tight all the way there.

The lift was crowded with people holding flowers and acting quiet and trying not to look at each other. Andy and me stood around while she spoke first to a nurse and then a doctor. Then she disappeared down a corridor for about half an hour, and came back looking worse than ever.

"Okay, we can all go in now," she said. "Just remember he's going to be all right – but he's a bit of a mess. Don't be frightened, okay, kids? And not too many questions."

So help me, it was a shock for all of us. I mean someone should have told us, to give us a chance. He was lying on his back in a ward with about five other patients. To be honest, I couldn't even recognise him. His whole face was swollen. He only had two narrow black slits to look out of. His nose looked like a lump of plasticine, and it had pieces of strapping around its base as if to hold it on. Purple and black bruising ran down one side of his face. When he saw Andy and me, he stared, but seemed scared to move his mouth. I felt like crying on the spot and I had to talk over this lump in my throat.

"Hi," he said between his teeth, with Andy hanging on to one of his hands. "Aren't I beautiful?"

"What happened?" Andy asked as if he couldn't believe it was for real.

"I hit a pole," he said, and it took him a long time.

On the way out in the lift, Jackie still didn't seem interested in talking. She just stood there looking at the other side of the lift, biting her lip, and I'd swear she even looked a bit angry about something.

Andy stood on the other side of her, looking around the lift as if in a space-capsule.

"Is his nose broken?" he asked.

"Yes," she said finally looking down at him.

But to tell you the truth, I was interested in other questions; like was Lesley Anherbrat in the car also at the time, and was she injured? And if he left the camp on Sunday, and had the accident last night, where was he or they in between? Jackie must have wondered about that too. But it was the wrong time for any of those questions with Alec being so bad. And another thing that was sticking in my memory was that on the left side of his head above his ear, he had a whole patch of hair missing as if it had been yanked out.

Wednesday July 15th

We all went to see Alec again tonight. I guess he was happy to see us, but he seemed to have no energy so we didn't stay long. If anything, I reckon he looked worse. The puffiness in his face was still there, and the bruises were going blue and red colours. And the more you looked the more damage you could see, like the scratches on his neck. Jackie said he should be home within a week because he's got nothing damaged on the inside.

I reckon I hardly heard one word the teachers said at school. And kids kept asking me all these dumb questions about the camp I had no answers for. About the only thing that was funny about the whole day was that Charlie got sprung in the dunnies smoking. A teacher from another Area who's a heavy caught him, and made him sweep out the toilets and that included the Girls' too. He had to do it because he was being blackmailed. The choice was either that or his mum being called up which gets real complicated because he promised her that he would never smoke because her father died of lung cancer.

I can't understand how some kids get so desperate for a cigarette. No kidding, some of them smoke walking to school, go to the dunnies for a fag as soon as they get there, and smoke every chance they get from then on during the day. And it's not that they're trying to be tough or anything because a lot of them go off by themselves to smoke. And you can tell the heavy smokers because they have to go to the toilet all the time during class. I reckon the teachers don't know how to stop it, or even help. Girls will tell teachers that they're having a period and they've got to rush to the toilet, and it's just for a fag, and the teacher really can't say no.

It's against the rules to smoke at school and yet if you go to the dunnies at the end of the day, the butts are piled up to the ceiling. And they reckon it's worse in the Girls'. I remember a couple of years ago it was real tough for a boy to smoke, especially at Primary school. Now you're a sort of hero if you're a boy and can give it up. We do a lot of talking in classes with the teachers about how bad it is for your health, and do experiments to show how much tar there is in a cigarette, and watch scary films of diseased lungs being cut up, but nothing changes, I don't reckon. And the teachers' staffroom is always full of smoke, so they've got the same problem. We had a 'Giving-Up Smoking' campaign at school and it included the teachers too. A kid was caught by another that same afternoon, and the teachers looked real relieved and went into the staffroom and had a meeting and talked about why the campaign had failed, and half of them were smoking.

Friday July 17th

Alec was the same tonight, still looking lifeless and in no mood to be hassled. The kids at school have already forgotten about the camp, although some from Alec's Area keep coming over and wanting to know when he will be back. I haven't seen any sign of Lesley Anherbrat all week, and I've been keeping my eye out.

Andy really freaked me this morning. It was one of those times when you're only about one percent awake, but that part is saying to your brain that you're being watched, and the next thing I was shooting up in bed, eyes open like a lighthouse. Andy was bending over the bed, just staring at me in the dark, and I thought he was awake because he started to whimper and said he wanted to go to the toilet.

"You know where to go," I said roughly because it wasn't

even dawn.

He repeated what he said and started hopping from one leg to the other. I thought he might be scared of the dark, so I said I would go with him.

"Hurry," he moaned.

I just had my dressing-gown on and was following him down the hallway, when I saw him go straight to the refrigerator, pull open the bottom vegetable-storage container and piss in it. I couldn't believe it.

"Hey," I said, but he had stopped moaning and his face looked peaceful in the light shining from the fridge. He slipped the container back into the fridge, walked straight past me as if I wasn't there, and went back to bed. I realised he was still asleep, sleep-walking.

Sunday July 19th

It's amazing. When we walked into the ward, it was Alec again. Overnight a lot of the swelling had gone and he was sitting up and able to talk. He got stuck into the orange-juice I carted in, and boy you should have seen how his hand shook when he held the glass. The rest of us ate his chocolate biscuits. Funny how his voice is shaky too, like he's not certain what he wants to say. The real good news was that he's coming home on Tuesday, and I reckon we can hardly wait for that. It's like we need him there to get things done properly, and I guess to take over when things are a worry. Like on the verandah last night.

We've had about five days straight of rain and cold winds, well up until yesterday afternoon. And funny thing, but when the rain stopped it also became calm and real mild weather for the middle of winter, so Andy and Jackie and me decided after tea to go out on the verandah and enjoy the freshness. In summer we used to sit out on the verandah as it grew dark, and watch all the people passing by in the street, and watch all the migrants sitting out on their front verandahs, and smell the trees and bushes, and try not to think of the dishes that still had to be done. Anyway we had only been out there a short time last night when a spider fell on to Jackie's hair as she was leaning against one of the verandah-posts. She got a real fright and shook her head hard because it dropped on to her lap. She brushed it off and went inside in a really foul mood and eventually went to bed early without even saying goodnight.

Tuesday July 21st

Alec was sitting in the sunroom talking to Andy when I got home from school. Andy was full of dumb questions, and it turned out that Alec also had two cracked ribs. The swelling has almost all disappeared and what is left is the dressing on his nose and bruises and scratches on his face and neck. I was a little bit nervous when I said hello as if he had been away for a million years and was now just a visitor.

"His body has had quite a shock," Jackie had said to me. "He'll be shaky for a while."

I told him about the kids in his Area asking after him. I don't know why, but he looked real sad about it.

"That's good," he said nodding his head as if he wasn't sure.

Wednesday July 22nd

We've got this Indian woman as our Science teacher. She's the smallest thing on two legs I've ever seen. And she's got this little stud which goes through one of her nostrils and her plaited hair falls to one side of her front, and it's so long I reckon she has trouble keeping it out of her food and from tripping over it. She hasn't got a very loud voice either, and when she wants to write something on the board, she's got to stand on a chair to begin with. She lets you make a lot of noise as long as you finish your work. One of the problems is that if you want to ask a question, you've got to look around the class for a while before you find her.

Anyway today we were cutting up dead rats and we were talking as normal when this guy who reckons he runs the Science Laboratory comes into the room and starts screaming at us for being too noisy. Sharmel, our teacher, said to him it was okay because we were cutting up rats. He sort of got a surprise at first because he hadn't seen her, and then had this look in his eyes as if he had worked out she couldn't be much of a teacher to have so much talking going on. So he ignored her and kept yelling at us. And he said to us who could tell him why we had to make so much noise. And I could see Charlie next to me was getting annoyed because he wanted to get on with pulling his rat's intestines out. So he started to say because we're cutting up rats. This guy then told Charlie to shut up and who had asked him to talk. And of course he had. All the time, Sharmel just stood there real quiet as if somehow this guy could help to get her the sack.

Friday July 24th

You know, when you look at Alec, it's like he was nice and safe and snug in a rest-home. He's also getting spoilt, like everyone hangs around him doing things to make things easier. Standing up and sitting down still seems to give him trouble because he does it in stages and holds his ribs at the same time. He also has real trouble getting into and out of bed. Jackie reckons it takes him about five minutes to get up in the morning, and in the morning is when his ribs hurt the most. His nose still hasn't healed as quick as the doctor thought, so he has trouble breathing, which means he gets sore throats from breathing through his mouth all the time, especially at night. Jackie's going to go crazy with his snoring.

"I bet you're missing school," I said, trying to help him get better quicker.

He didn't say anything for the moment, but his mood had completely changed.

"You'd better know, Mark," he said quietly. "I won't be going back to my teaching job."

"Why not?" I asked, getting used to shocks.

He seemed to be trying to be real careful what he said. "I did a lot of thinking in hospital; I think fourteen years is too long to teach."

"You'll change your mind," I said, because I'd heard it all before. And then somehow I found the courage to ask him about the camp. I told him what the kids said about him rescuing Lesley Anherbrat.

"What happened?" I asked him.

He looked upwards and his eyes glazed a little and he rubbed his forehead with his palm like he had a headache.

"It got out of hand," he said trying to control his voice.

"Where did you go after the camp?" I said, carefully.

He sat there staring at the garden outside, and suddenly I realised he wasn't going to answer. And he didn't look young and strong any more.

Sunday July 26th

At tea tonight, Jackie said she was going to be a teacher again.

"I applied for registration as an Emergency Teacher today," she said, looking straight at Alec. "I have an interview at a Footscray school tomorrow."

"I'll start looking for a job in the morning," he said, looking unhappy.

"You know you can't yet," she answered. "I'll fit it in

93

with the design work. It'll only be temporary."

She then looked at Andy and me: "These two squirts don't need me any more."

"It's shit work," Alec said, still looking glum.

Monday July 27th

This kid came to class this morning with a woollen beany pulled down over his ears. He didn't say anything and wouldn't let anyone wear his cap.

"Take your hat off, George," Paul Kelly said for fun.

He shook his head and so a kid behind him snatched it off. His head had been shaven like one of those Buddhist monks. It turned out that his dad didn't like the friends he had been mixing with so shaved George's hair off and made him sleep under the bed.

I saw Alec at school too. He was walking slowly and carefully through the doors of the Administration block. He must have been going to see the Principal about his leaving teaching. No kidding, no one tells you anything any more.

Wednesday July 29th

"There now, try and make me laugh and see if it hurts," said Alec to both of us.

Andy went cross-eyed and pulled out his mouth with his thumbs. I reckon he looked better. Then he got up and walked like an ape around the table and stuck his face in Alec's.

"You've got to make me laugh, though," stirred Alec.

Andy and me have been trying to make him laugh because we know it hurts his ribs. It's just a game, and anyway everyone reckons he's better.

Andy crept up behind his chair and pulled a hair out.

"That was a white one," he said to Alec. "I can count tons of those; you must be getting old."

And that didn't seem to make Alec laugh either.

He's got a bump on his nose which wasn't there before. Alec said they may have to break it again sometime and do a better job. I offered to do it for him.

And that didn't make him laugh.

Sunday August 2nd

There was low talking coming from their bedroom last night. Opposite me, Andy was breathing real strange and gurgling and muttering to himself like dogs do when they dream. Anyway, I sneaked up the hallway hardly breathing myself. It was real difficult to hear what they were saying because the door was shut.

Alec said something like: "That's just how the law works sometimes . . ."

And Jackie said: "I suppose it's lucky in a way . . ."

Then Alec said something about a deal outside because of the assault charges.

I reckon they must have heard the floorboards creak a little because there was no talking at all after that, just whispering.

I sneaked back to bed and lay awake for hours thinking about the words 'assault charges'. They hung over me like huge weights in my brain and made my heart beat real hard sometimes. Who assaulted who? Was Alec really in an accident, or did that escaped convict, Lesley Anherbrat's uncle, beat him up? And why would he beat Alec up? What would he have against Lesley's teacher, except perhaps he was jealous of her having a crush on Alec? But why did Alec drive off at the camp? I mean he never solved problems like that. And where did they go that night? And then right in the middle of these thoughts I went cold. What if the assault charges were against Alec? That he was discovered having sex with Lesley Anherbrat in a motel room or something. That would be real bad, because she's only young. But that was impossible. I mean he's got Jackie, and a family. He wouldn't be so dumb, so dirty. I knew he just wouldn't do it, even if he was always talking about people not owning each other. Why don't they talk about it? They just close up if ever I ask any questions. Now I'm embarrassed to. But if there's something important going on, I have a right to know. I'm one of the family, aren't I?

I lay thinking about that over and over again, and the fact no one had hardly made a fuss about me turning fifteen today; until finally I heard the clink of milk bottles and fell asleep.

Monday August 3rd

Uncle Liam leaned over the fence and stared at the front garden. He's fascinated by the large number of trees we planted in a small space.

"Well, there you are," he said laughing to himself. Then he turned serious. "And how would ya pa be coming along, young fella?"

"All right," I said unconvincingly.

He put his kit-bag down and leaned closer to me. I could smell beer on his breath, and he sure looked grey.

"Just between you and me," he said quietly, "ya pa's one of these fellas that was born with a nest of hornets up his trouser leg."

I hadn't heard this one.

"What do you mean?" I asked him.

"He was smitten with a restless spirit," he said, cocking his head sideways to see if I understood. "I've seen fellas just like him wandering the hills, roving out; never being able to recognise happiness which is right there in front of their noses. These fellas have always gotta be doin' some-thin'. They're afraid to stop, like they might find somethin' out about themselves."

He gave me this long knowing look, then lifted one hand up in his salute.

"Ah well," he said, "I best be trippin' along. Me missus will have the spuds on. Say hello to ya ma, and to the wee-fella that will be famous one day."

And he laughed to himself, and went to pick up his bag.

"Do you know anything about how the law works?" I asked him. He seemed about the only person I could ask without attracting suspicion. I couldn't talk to Paul Kelly because he knew Alec.

"Well that would depend," Uncle Liam said cocking his head forward. "Try me."

I stalled a moment, feeling stupid about what I was going to ask.

"What happens to someone who has sex with young girls?" I said trying to sound casual.

He stuck his face right in mine, and looked at me closely.

"Well that would depend upon how old the lassie is who's been messed with," he said. "If she t'wer under the age of consent then it's a crime of the land. That would be called carnal knowledge."

"And how would you know what under-aged is?" I said.

"Ah well," he thought, taking out his tobacco tin. "I wouldn't be certain of that. About fifteen in this country I would say."

"Aha," I said. "Is it a serious crime . . . you know, jail and all that?"

"It can be for sure," he answered, fumbling a cigarette together. "It has pulled great men down."

"Well I reckon it must happen all the time," I said. "They wouldn't be able to look everyone up."

"True," he said, and there seemed to be anger in his voice.

He was staring right into my eyes with his watery ones.

"I'm sure the powers of authority are lenient on those young'uns that have been messin' with one another. But have ye thought of having to march down the aisle before ya time and in disgrace of your family; and someone else more powerful is knowing of such crimes, and mayn't be as lenient."

He must have thought I'd got some girl pregnant.

Tuesday August 4th

Alec has been looking through the papers for a job each day. Saturday seemed real important to him. He was up early and sat over the breakfast table for a long time drawing biro marks next to different telephone numbers. It seemed only to make him unhappy though, as if he was getting confused.

He tried the Employment Service today with no luck. You can tell he's getting restless; he can't keep still, walks around the block a lot and is always dropping things. He sure doesn't like doing nothing. And you should see how his hands shake sometimes.

Wednesday August 5th

I can't see how come the school canteen is allowed to sell us food which is stale and cold and badly cooked, and makes kids vomit. It's as if only kids are eating it so it doesn't matter. I mean that's how we're treated. The teachers are served at a different section, and their food always looks fresher or hotter. Some of us complained to Paul Kelly, but he said the school had given some sort of contract to the guy running the canteen, so nothing could be done. He reckons if you want healthy food, then bring it from home. I reckon kids would like to eat healthy food if given the chance. And it's no good teachers telling us all about balanced diets and all that crap when they don't do anything about the canteen.

Thursday August 6th

I stayed home from school today because I've got a cold. Alec went out during the morning checking out two jobs, and it was Jackie's first day Emergency teaching. When Alec got home I watched him around the house. Funny, he did a lot of cleaning up, you know, house-work, in slow-motion; and no kidding, the house is never a mess any more. And he cooks nearly every night now, but hardly eats. He just sits there and drinks red wine and chain smokes. Funny though, you never see him doing anything in the garden any more or fixing the house up. I can remember it wasn't long ago that he would have given a million dollars to have the free time he has now, to do work on the house.

Anyway we did some talking in the afternoon, and I reckon it's the first time we've really talked for a few months. We talked about how things had changed in the world. Alec talked about the kids he went to school with – what they were like, and the tricks they got up to. Things like crawling down enormous water-drains; playing games with strange names like 'saddle-me-nag', 'Charlie-over-the-water', 'kiss-chasy', 'cherry-bobbing', and 'alleys and tors'. And they used to camp out in the backyard in tents they rigged up themselves out of old canvas, they did up bikes, sneaked looks through their parents' medical encyclo-paedias, tooth-pasted their neighbours' door-knobs, kept away from girls and got gravel-rashes from playing footy and piggy-back fights, lost their lunch-money to the school bullies, had secret-code clubs, put on pantomimes that the neighbours had to pay to see, drew lines on their faces with lipstick to look like American Indians, had explosions in back-sheds from mixing the wrong chemicals of their secret

99

formula for eternal youth, invented war-games and musical instruments. And the kids he described all had nicknames like 'Rocka', 'Jorgo', 'Gus', 'Aggot', and 'Willy', and they all just about lived together day and night.

And then I said that even though I had just turned fifteen, just in a couple of years I had seen things change. Like I remembered when no one could afford their own watches and skates; when people didn't go around saying you'd go sterile if you wore tight jeans; when you didn't have to worry about no jobs and pollution and cancer all the time; and computers; and sex seemed a lot more dirty to talk about. I told Alec that even the first years that arrived at school weren't innocent little kids any more, like some of the girls seemed to be crazy nymphomaniacs, even did the asking if they wanted to go with you. And you had to be careful what you said about sex because it had all been talked about in class discussions, and if you said the wrong thing, some girl was liable to turn around and tell you that you didn't know what you're talking about and suggest some book you can find in the library to help you.

And I told Alec that I thought people acted like they were blind half the time, that they didn't seem to notice what was going on around them. Like you see awful things going on in the streets and on trams and things, but people around acted like it wasn't really happening – especially older people.

And I told him about some kids I'd known at school. There was Jeff in the first year who was called 'the Dog' because he used to hide under the desks in class and bark and snap at people, and his poems were all about monsters ripping people apart. Then there was John who still cried about his dog that was poisoned when he was four – ten years ago. And I know a brother and sister who throw cats off the top of the flats, and kids who look like they haven't eaten for years; and kids I reckon who have brain damage from late-night movies each night because they are afraid to go to sleep because their parents don't come home; and kids who sometimes have talked about living in derelict buildings and lanes with their other little brothers and sisters.

"You see what's going on," said Alec. "I'm impressed."

He said it in a way that made me feel proud. So then I asked him if he had any sorts of problems he wanted to share with me because I might be able to help. It was like a dark cloud went over the house. He frowned, and couldn't seem to look at me after that, and after a short time got up and went for a walk.

Wednesday August 12th

There's this kid who arrived about four weeks ago at our school. We call him 'Roly-Poly' because he likes to roll all the time – like side-rolls and forward somersaults. It's like the top half of his body is too heavy and he feels most relaxed when rolling along. He does it on lino, grass, concrete, in the canteen, and in the classroom. You've just got to touch him and straight away he'll do a roll, or if you even touch the back of his chair, he'll roll off it. And when he's finished his roll, he will always come up smiling, and I reckon everyone else smiles too, like he's some sort of entertainer. When he first arrived he seemed an unhappy kid, but in just a few weeks was acting real confident. I reckon he goes out of his way to find hairs and ants and dust to trip over, just so he can do a roll. He loves PE because he can just roll all the time. There's always opportunities in PE. He hasn't got a dad and his mother has shifted he reckons about five times in two years. So this was his third school this year. Anyway he hasn't been at school this week and today we learnt that he had left.

I also got told that Lesley Anherbrat has left, which explains why I haven't been able to notice her since Alec's accident. This kid reckons she's shifted too – she lived in his street.

"Everyone reckons she was a real moll," he said. "And too big for her boots. But she always said goodaye to me when she went past, and was real friendly like.

Thursday August 13th

Alec starts a job tomorrow. He reckons he got it through a combination of lies and luck. He's going to be driving a delivery-van around all day, taking lollies and chocolate orders to shops.

"Can't wait to start," he said to all of us at tea. "Just what I've been waiting for. An outdoor job and the chance to meet a whole lot of new people. It was made for me."

I reckon it's a waste. He should be teaching; and I can tell Jackie thinks that too. But she didn't say anything.

Friday August 14th

A real bad thing happened at school today. Billy got chucked out. Mr Whiles, the metal-work teacher, who really loves himself just because he's good looking and he reckons all the girls are in love with him, was responsible. The only thing he does is look out the window, or act bored, or say sarcastic things to kids he doesn't like. Sometimes he picks on kids just because they're fat or they can't read properly or don't finish in time.

"Come on, you big pudding, haven't you finished yet?" he said to this Turkish girl who is really big. She dropped her head down, and you could see the tears actually falling from her face, and her nose and mouth were running too.

"Come on, stop blubbering, you're not home now with your mother there to wipe your bottom," he said, and when he said it, he looked around with a grin on the side of his mouth, and a couple of sucks laughed too, but mainly it was quiet.

"Leave her alone, suck," Billy said under his breath.

"And you pull your head in, Strachan," Whiles said with a sort of bored voice but staring straight at Billy.

"You made her cry," Billy answered keeping his eyes on the desk in front of him.

"I'm not blind Strachan; obviously she hasn't a sense of humour," and he gestured with his head towards the door and his face was a little red. "And now I want you to do us all a favour and take your horrible little face away from here," he said.

"Why should I?" Billy always says that to teachers. "I haven't done anything wrong."

"Get out, Strachan, or I'll throw you out."

Billy continued to look at the desk. I reckon he was getting pretty emotional.

"Why should I?" he said real quietly.

Whiles walked up behind Billy and pushed two fingers and a thumb into Billy's neck which made him throw his head back and screw his face up. Whiles made him stand up by lifting his grip and then led him to the door and, opening it with his other hand, threw him out. He then closed the door again and dusted his hands off. I could see that Billy was really flipping when he got dragged out, and that it wouldn't be the end of it. He just can't handle being pushed around. The door flew open again, and Billy looked around the room half-laughing and half-crying.

"Leave me alone you fucking poofta," he screamed.

While's lips started to shake and I reckon he was having trouble controlling himself too; it was like all of a sudden these two people were old enemies or something. Billy didn't seem to know what to do next either. He stuck his middle finger up in the air at the teacher.

"You wait. My big brother's going to shoot you," he said. "And you can stick your school up your arse," and I think he tried to break the glass in the door, because he slammed it as hard as he could and ran off.

Mr Whiles stared for a moment as if he couldn't believe he'd been spoken to like that.

"Strachan's vocabulary isn't going to take him far now that he's left school, I'm afraid," he said, and you could tell from his face that he was trying to act cool, but the shake in his voice gave him away, and then he went to the Office.

Billy was hanging around after school. He said his parents had been told that he was expelled, but he didn't give a shit, even though his dad would bash him when he got home. He reckons he sneaked out to see us.

When I got home tonight, I told Alec what had happened. I wanted him to help get Billy back into school.

"Billy's got to want to," he said.

"But it was Mr Whiles' fault. He started it," I said.

"There's thousands of teachers like Brian Whiles," said Alec, looking unhappy. "Unfortunately, for their own reasons, they don't like children and yet still choose to become teachers."

Saturday August 15th

Billy rang up this afternoon and said there's no way he's coming back to school. He didn't get a beating either because his old man got pissed last night and when he woke up this morning said it was a good thing and that Billy had to get a job. His mum cried, though. I suddenly realised that I was old enough to get a job too, and that I was no longer protected by school. But whatever could I do?

Jackie also organised a dinner party for some friends last night. When I say friends, they were mainly teachers Alec had taught with. Normally the guests arrive later than they said they would, and they all bring bottles of wine under their arms, and Alec will already have a flagon opened, so the bottles mount up in the fridge, but Alec reckons they're handy for when you visit other people's houses for dinner parties. And they usually always end up talking about teaching and politics, so Andy and me either watch TV or try and say smart things at the table, or I go off to Charlie's place. And they usually stay up pretty late drinking and smoking, and pot after pot of coffee is brewed, and everyone reckons they have to work tomorrow so they had better be going soon, but they don't.

Last night was different though. They all arrived on time, except three people who rang to say they couldn't make it; no one seemed to want to talk about teaching, it was quiet all night as if they were all strangers all of a sudden; and two of them said they had to get up early in the morning to go up country, and when that happened the other two said they'd better go too, and suddenly even though it was still early the dinner party was over. Alec didn't seem to care but Jackie looked both angry and disappointed.

Sunday August 16th

I haven't heard the radio turned up loud in Alec and Jackie's room, or those strangling sounds since he's been out of hospital. Don't they do it any more?

Monday August 17th

Most kids at school wouldn't be seen dead with their mums. Their mums are always doing real dumb things right out in the open in the street where anyone's mates might be, like trying to take their arm to cross the road, and licking their handkerchiefs to get stains off the kid's shirt, things like that. It's funny seeing the tough kids from school looking real dopy and being led around doing the shopping by their mums Saturday mornings. They try and fall behind as if they're really doing the shopping by themselves, but you can always see their mums because they're always about three metres in front of them, turned around, waving their hands with the hurry-up signal, or rushing back and dragging them along by the arm.

Jackie doesn't pull any of those stunts. She acts as if it's up to me whether I want to tag along or not. Usually I do because I like the places she goes to, but when she starts looking through materials and bargains and secondhand stuff, I usually head for the closest record shop.

Wednesday August 19th

To be honest, I reckon there have been secrets going on in our house since Alec's accident. You don't have to be real smart to notice that there's more whispering going on and that conversations are dropped when you walk into the room. We've always talked things over at tea-time and thinking back I can't remember any whispering – except perhaps Andy and me in the middle of the night, but that's different. Normally I could ask them anything I wanted to, but how do you ask your parents how come they've started keeping secrets? It's as if you've got no right to because you're a kid.

Now it's often dead quiet at the table and you can hear people chewing their food, and you can tell that Jackie and Alec are talking about nothing just to get a conversation going. Even Andy's getting into the habit of playing with his food with his fork. Sometimes when it's quiet you can hear his breathing fading away like a bell. And he's had a couple of bad attacks of asthma lately, and Jackie's had him at the doctor's twice.

Alec and Jackie still hug each other, but it's not like the wrestling and playing around that I was used to seeing.

Now when they hug, it's only occasionally and it's like they're clinging to each other as if the house was on fire.

What I really hate is hearing their voices talking low in the loungeroom or bedroom when Andy and me are in bed. Last night I got up because I wanted to have a piss, and as I was about to pass the loungeroom, I heard Alec's voice which sounded croaky and he was talking about two policemen in the Principal's Office at school. As I passed the door, the light was real blinding and they were both sitting on the couch together and Jackie had her arm around his shoulder and his eyes were bloodshot.

I said real sleepily: "Why are you two still up?" I must have given Jackie a fright.

"What are you doing up?" she snapped angrily at me.

"Going to the toilet," I sort of whinged. "It's a free world isn't it?"

"Don't worry, mate," Alec croaked softly, "We're going to bed soon."

Monday August 24th

When I got home I discovered that Alec had given up his job.

"I made up my mind on the spot," he said. "I parked the van, rang the firm and told them where they could find it and the keys; and then walked home free as a bird."

Jackie looked unimpressed. "Just like that?" she said.

Thursday August 27th

Alec's getting into wandering around the house in the middle of the night. If he goes to bed before midnight, you can predict he's going to be up later. You'll hear him in the kitchen making cups of tea, or in the loungeroom. It puts you off, as if he's leading a life that begins when yours ends for the day. He might get up and go back to bed about three or four times during the night. Sometimes you can hear him going off for a walk, and I don't know why but that can really keep you awake because you start listening for his footsteps to return, echoing from the footpath in the quiet street. It's only then that you can go to sleep. Sometimes it makes me feel real angry, like why does he have to get up all the time and keep everybody else awake. Inconsiderate I'd call it. He's such a nervous person now. Jesus, I just hope Jackie is a good sleeper. I guess it's not his fault really. I reckon he's just not used to doing nothing during the day, and so his mind isn't tired out.

Tuesday September 1st

Since it's the holidays, I decided to go and visit Billy tonight to see how he's getting on. Funny, I've known him for a whole year and yet never been to his place. He lives in the Housing Commission Flats. Inside the foyer on the ground floor I ran my eyes down the list of residents. The name Strachan was against the number 104 and on level nine. The foyer was crowded and noisy. There were some kids my age arguing about some fags; a Turkish family stood like a family photograph waiting for the lift with their pram; two fat ladies with hair-curlers in and packets of milk and newspapers under their arms were talking loudly. I don't reckon the foyer was supposed to be comfortable. The rough plaster on the walls had yellowed, the lino was grotty, and the darkness of the stairwells and letter-box made the whole thing look real bare.

And once we were all crammed inside the lift, you could see names and dates scratched all over its walls and there was this sickly disinfectant smell about it. One of the big women had taken over the floor-buttons as if the lift was hers.

"Whaddya want, luv?" she asked me.

She pressed nine for me and then five for herself. The husband of the Turkish family waited until everyone had finished pushing, then stepped forward and pressed their number and then back again into a corner where his family was gathered. I tried smiling at them, but they looked blank at me.

The corridor leading to Flat 104 was totally exposed to the outside weather. When I looked over the balcony I could see this fantastic view of the city skyline and its sparkling lights. It was different though when I looked over the edge: the further down you looked, the smaller the flats seemed to get and I got this fear that they might topple over. Distant sounds of screaming children floated up through the still air from the ground level, and the roar of traffic never stopped. I wondered how on earth Superman would ever find the guts to jump off a building like this.

I pressed the doorbell and a voice screamed from inside: "Well, answer it."

Someone struggled on the inside to turn the knob, and finally the door was half opened and a small face peered round it and said: "Yes?"

"Billy home?" I asked back.

The small face stared back at me real serious.

"Just a minute," it said, then slipped off into the room.

"Billy, there's a man to see you," I heard her say. And then her face reappeared around the door and she said: "He won't be long."

But she didn't go away. She just stood there and stared. Billy came to the door holding on to another little kid on his hip. When he saw me his face really brightened up. He sure was rapt.

"Hey man," he said. "Come in."

The funny thing about flats is that you think there could be only one room the way their front doors are lined up like that. We walked past a kitchen into the living-room. Two more small kids jumped out of bed and followed me into the room. The flat was amazingly clean. In one corner was this huge rubber-tree plant, and there was this three hundred inch colour TV set stuck in the other corner, and two older boys were slouched in armchairs watching it. But Billy was jumping all around me.

"How you been, man?" he asked with his hand on my shoulder.

"That's Mae," he said pointing to the little girl who had answered the door. "And that's Graham and Brian, they're me brother's mates, and that's Gail and . . ." he hugged the little child on his hip . . . "this is Rendy, our little princess."

And then his mother was fished out of the bathroom to meet me and she seemed to be as happy to see me as Billy was, and she started running around buttering biscuits and making hot chocolate. She must be one of the smallest women I've seen, and her hair is stone white and her skin looks like it's been stretched over bones wet and then let dry. I was made to feel like some lost brother returned home.

Billy dragged me around the flat showing me all the things they owned and especially what was his. I began to get embarrassed because it was like he was trying to prove something.

"And I once saw a person fall past this window," said Billy still smiling and leading me over to the living-room window. "Some crazy dame on the fifteenth floor threw her babies off the balcony and then jumped."

I was sat down on the couch and given three plates of different kinds of biscuits and a mug of hot chocolate. Billy's mum stood back against a wall and watched me. I asked her if she was going to have something and she said they had just had tea. So had I. The two guys watching TV never looked up once.

"Wanna see my colouring-book?" I think it was Gail said to me, holding onto my smallest finger. She rushed off to get it when I smiled. Gail came back with the book and stood on the couch in her pyjamas next to me. This other little kid was on my other side hugging onto my arm as if I might leave. I flipped through the pages of the book and noticed that everything was coloured in except for people. I did an adult trick and said it was great. She giggled and accidentally kicked me in the balls as she raced off.

No kidding, I began to feel right at home after a while, and Billy told me about how he couldn't find a job and his mum just stood around smiling as if Billy was in charge, and he was even the one who told two of the young ones they had to go to bed. I never guessed Billy could be like that. Everything was going great until his dad got home.

"Don't take any notice of the bastard," Billy said to me.

A lot of loud talking came into the flat. Billy's dad was a big man with an enormous gut. His face was bright red with veins running all around his nose. Under one arm he held a box of beer bottles. He had two friends with him, and with the three of them standing in the middle of the room, things were getting pretty crowded. And they made it smell like a brewery. One of the others was an older guy who looked like a dried-out nectarine. The third person was a fat reddish woman who was still puffing from the ride in the elevator. She was carrying a handbag that looked like a bucket. She looked around the room and smiled as if she was some sort of health inspector.

"Hello luv," she said to Billy's mum. "Haven't you got the place looking nice."

Then Billy's mum all of a sudden came alive.

"Yeah, and no one could guess where you've been all day," she said to his dad.

He was taking out a fold-up card-table, and organising drinks for his guests.

"Make yourself useful," he said to her. "Get off your butt and make us some coffee."

"Get ya friends to make it," she answered.

I've got to hand it to her, she had guts, with him standing

111

there a foot away, breathing beer down at her.

Then he said something about her earning her house-keeping money for a change, and that he didn't know why he bothered sticking around, and I don't know how, but all of a sudden everyone was screaming, including Billy and the guests, and his dad for no reason punched his mum in the face as hard as anything. But she kept at it even though there was blood on her lip, and I just sat quiet as a mouse on the couch with Mae who had the little princess on her lap, and she was really hugging that child hard. At some stage Billy managed to say to me that I'd better go. So I did.

And right now even, I keep thinking of the Turkish family sitting at a meal together, perhaps on the floor below, listening to the noises above. And I still see that look in Mae's eyes as she hugged the little princess.

Wednesday September 2nd

Last night all of a sudden, I woke up feeling really alert as if everything wasn't right. I looked at the clock which showed 3:45am, and I also noticed a little bit of light coming from underneath the door. I got up and wandered down the hall-way, and saw that the light was coming from the lounge-room. I looked in, and there was Alec lying asleep on the couch. I reckon if I had had a blanket or something, I could have thrown it over him. I was sort of shivering in the cold air myself so I decided I should wake him. But before I had moved, he suddenly sat up and stared at me. No kidding, with his long legs and arms, and drooped forward on the couch, he looked like one of those bloody spiders outside.

"Aren't you going to bed, Alec?" I sort of whispered across to him.

He didn't say anything; he just looked at me, so I thought maybe he was somehow still asleep, so I left him and went to bed. Those sheets and blankets sure felt good. Shortly after I heard him turn the light off and go to their room.

Thursday September 3rd

Alec went and asked for a dish-washing job in an Italian restaurant in Carlton, and got it. In fact they said he could start straight away tonight. So while I'm writing this, and it's 9:30pm, Alec will be in the middle of his new job.

Saturday September 5th

This new job of Alec's is sort of good and bad. It's good because if you're up to see him get home, you can tell he's really shagged and so far he's gone straight to bed. He's even sleeping in late in the mornings which is not like him because he reckons he's just like his dad was, and grandfather, and great-grandfather; he has to be up at the crack of dawn. The bad part about it is when school starts we'll just never see him, except for about an hour after school maybe. And even then he's been going off in the afternoons by himself and getting home just in time to go off to work. I reckon I'll see him less than some of the kids at school who see their parents after factory jobs. I told him that, and he said it would only go on for a little while longer. Does that mean he's planning to go back to teaching?

Monday September 7th

Uncle Liam had a stroke at work and is in hospital. Jackie and me went down to see his wife. He's not allowed to have any visitors. You could tell she was trying to be real brave by the way she was biting her handkerchief. You know it was the first time I had really heard her talking. She made about eight cups of tea and talked about her Liam and herself and how they met when he was selling vegetables from door to door, and she brought out pictures of them over the years and said their only child had died in his cot, and Liam never wanted children after that. And I told her Liam was too tough for anything to go wrong. And Jackie agreed and held her hand. She went on to say how he only had a few years before he retired, and that they found him at work slumped over his desk. And the first time she went to visit him, he said he had to get out of the place because he was surrounded by Masons at the hospital, and that one of the doctors had the fire in his eyes; and the next day she went to visit him, they had put tubes up his nose and in his arm, and he didn't know it was her. Anyway we were in the kitchen talking and it started to get dark, and Jackie and me said we'd better go, and she said she had to go back to the hospital. She's a real nice lady, and yet before this afternoon, she'd always been Mrs McNamara with the broken hip and stick who lives down the street.

Tuesday September 8th

Alec came home pissed tonight. We had been waiting for about two hours to start tea, so everyone was in a bad mood when he got home. He kept saying, "What's wrong?" to all of us in turn and was talking real loud and then would quite suddenly stop as if he had heard himself. Jackie dished all our meals up without saying anything, and he kept talking loudly all the way through it, and most of it was all about himself and how you had to love yourself before you could love others.

I reckon the first thing Jackie said since he had come home was: "What about the restaurant?"

Her voice sounded cold.

"What restaurant?" he said and sort of started giggling

as if there was something funny about what he said. She
didn't say anything in return. She just got up and went into
the loungeroom and closed the door in a way that said no
one else better follow her. Andy and me cleared the dishes
away and washed up and didn't say anything; and Alec just
sat at the table real quiet.

Finally he said as if he was sorry: "Of course I'm going to
the restaurant."

And he got up and walked out. I wondered standing there
drying the dishes who he'd been drinking with. I don't
reckon Jackie knows either. He could have at least rung up.

Wednesday September 9th

This morning Andy crawled into bed with me and got down
under the sheets and hugged my leg. I could feel his throat
pulse racing against my hip. It started to ache and my leg
get pins-and-needles, so I got him out and let him hug my
back.

"What's wrong?" I asked.

"Nothin'," he spat into my ear, and then he mumbled
that he had had another nightmare. He wouldn't tell me
what it was about though.

We lay there for a while, and I was just about to drop off
to sleep again, when he said: "What's going to happen?"

"Whaddya mean?" I said, nearly in another world.

I remember him sniffing a bit.

"He doesn't like us any more," he whispered.

That really woke me up. I knew who he was talking about. .

"Why do you say that?" I asked.

"They don't act like they used ta," he answered. "And he
never wants to know what I'm doin' any more. And he never
reads me books any more."

"Don't be a dag," I said. "He's our dad. You want to see
Billy's. He bashes his mum. Alec's just unhappy because

115

he's not teaching. He still loves you."

"Promise?" he said sniffing.

"Of course I promise," I said, hoping he wouldn't feel my heart beating hard.

We lay there a moment, and he was probably wondering about what we'd said also.

"Alec's girlfriend wouldn't let me into our house," he said quietly.

"What?" I asked, sounding real surprised.

"In the dream. She wouldn't let me in. She said I didn't live here any more."

I told him it was only a dream, and everything would be okay when the sun came up. And then I had a good idea. I challenged him to a game of drawing numbers on each other's backs and guessing the number, just like we used to do in the bath using soap; so we played it, whispering in the night's silence until daylight came around. He finally drifted off and so did I for an hour or two. When I woke up, he was back in his own bed.

"I hate that bitch," he said, turning to me.

Thursday September 10th

Billy's been hanging around the school a lot. Sometimes he even comes into the Canteen at lunchtime, even though he's not supposed to. You can tell he's got nothing to do and just hangs around the streets all day. He would be better off at school I reckon.

"Hah," he will say. And then he starts talking about getting Whiles back and some of the other teachers. But he always asks about a lot of the kids and what we're doing and then wanders off by himself down the street at the end of lunchtime.

Friday September 11th

We're doing this work at the moment at school on what happens to food after you swallow it. Anyway it's kind of fascinating, so I decided to do my homework straight away when I got home. But I couldn't work out on the handout about juices from other parts of your body mixing with the food in your stomach. It was confusing. One minute there's arrows showing these things being added to the food, and on the other hand arrows showing things being taken out of the food. So I asked Alec who was home to give me a hand, and he came out into the sunroom and we went over it together. The only problem was it didn't change anything. I still couldn't understand what was coming or going. And I said so, even though I felt real dumb and when he didn't answer me I looked up at him. He hadn't even been listening. He was just staring out of the window a million miles away. And at first I couldn't work out the expression on his face; then it hit me. He looked lonely.

Sunday September 13th

I hadn't been in bed long last night when I got up to get some water because of a sore throat. I just struggled out half-asleep like you do without bothering to turn any lights on. On the way back to the bedroom, I walked into the light of the moon that shone through the glass surrounds of the front door. A large spider was hanging between the hall-stand and the opposite wall. I reckon it must have been no more than ten centimetres in front of my nose. I turned the light on and killed it with a rolled-up newspaper. I can't work out how I didn't walk into it on the way to the kitchen.

Thursday September 17th

The last four days have been pretty desperate. I suppose it

was a shock because it didn't seem possible; but it was possible ever since he got out of hospital. Funny, but I've felt a bit empty since then. I've been hopeless at school and it's hard to keep trying all the time at home. All I can do is describe what it was like.

Monday was an overcast day, but from the moment I stepped in the back door, I felt the cold and grey. Jackie sat there in the shadow, her eyes and nose red raw, a tea saucer of butts on the arm of the chair, and she just stared out into the garden.

"Alec's gone to Queensland," she said, and tears started rolling down her face.

"Whaddya mean?" I said.

Her lip curled under.

"He packed and left at lunchtime," she said, her voice breaking a little.

"Why's he gone to Queensland? Where will he stay? Is he trying to get work?"

She shrugged her shoulders as if she couldn't understand anything any more.

"When's he gonna come back?" I asked, beginning to feel pretty desperate.

"I don't know," she said, shaking her head. "And at the moment don't fucking care if he never comes back."

And just then I heard Andy come in behind us and drop his bag down.

"Where's Dad?" he said, and his eyes had suspicion in them.

So she repeated what she'd told me, except by now you could hardly hear what she was saying; and he asked exactly the same questions until finally she disappeared into the bathroom for about one hour. She took us out to a restaurant for tea, which was noisy and crowded, probably to get us away from the quietness of the house, but no one ate much. It was like he had died.

Anyway Alec rang on Tuesday night from Sydney, and

spoke to all of us in turn. Jackie was real short with him, and when I got on he started talking about how much he still loved us, but that he needed a break and couldn't live a lie any more, and to be honest I couldn't understand any of it and wasn't really listening; I was just enjoying his voice. He said something about how it wasn't the end of us as a family of friends, and I guess I didn't know what to say to that. And when I handed it to Andy, the words began to sink in, and suddenly I froze. For the first time I realised that he had left us and that he wasn't talking about coming back.

Since then my mind has been going crazy. I keep asking myself why he's left us. Is he on the run from the cops for having sex with Lesley Anherbrat? Did *we* do something wrong? Is he going insane? Does he know what he's doing to us? Jackie is going bananas; Andy's going around like a zombie; and I've never felt so bad at any other time in my life. I just feel empty all the time; and the real joke is I don't know why my father has pissed off to Queensland. What am I supposed to tell other people?

Do you know what I thought about all last night in bed? Whether Alec ever really loved me. And when I start thinking like that my mind goes crazy, and I start to hate him, and then I want to run and find him, like in one of those dumb novels we've read at school where fourteen-year-old kids go and rescue their kidnapped dad. But the truth is I'm paralysed by my thinking. And then I start thinking that I'll never forgive him, and then wonder if he'll give us another chance. And I try to imagine what he might be doing and whether he wants me to stay with him for a while. And then something dumb happens because I get real scared that he might leave the country or find another family or even commit suicide.

But more and more I see him as being selfish because how could whatever he wants to do be more important than being with us. That's why I think he's either in trouble, or maybe he never loved us at all.

I conned Charlie into wagging Activities this afternoon, and we went and played the pinball machines at a café near the school.

"Do you trust your parents?" I asked him.

"Why not?" he said, looking surprised at my dumb question. "They just don't trust me and my sister."

"They seem good to me," I said.

He whacked the machine hard he was on.

"They're always inviting these jerks around with their parents to look over Silvana, like she's some sort of horse being checked over before being sold," he said. "And they're always asking me what work I'm doing at school; who my friends are; whether I take drugs. They think they own us just because they came to Australia to give us an education. I tell you. They're still living in Sicily."

"Whaddya expect from them," I said, sounding a bit angry.

He kept staring at me, as if I had gone nuts.

"Nothing," he said. "Just to be trusted and left alone, and my sister too. If they had their way, I'd end up living with them all my life."

We moved on and started playing a couple of harder machines. I was nearly out of coins.

"That's why *your* parents are so great, you lucky sod," he went on. "They trust you and treat you like an adult and a friend. You don't realise how bloody lucky you are.

Is your dad still working in that spaghetti place?" he said to me when we were outside.

I guess he was the first person to ask me that question.

"No," I said. "He's got a job in Queensland teaching for a couple of months."

"See what I mean?" Charlie said. "My old man couldn't trust leaving us for a week."

Sunday September 20th

I guess the things you don't want to think about always come back at night. You're okay during the day as long as you keep running. But in bed at night, the house is dead still and my mind is wide awake. I reckon someone could go mad if it kept going like that; or at least you'd need a jar of sleeping-pills next to the bed.

I always hope to drift off straight away, but the longer I lie there, the more awake I become. I hear things like dripping taps; the fridge's motor changing rhythm; Andy's breathing; the ticking of his travelling clock with its traffic-cop's hands; and, no kidding, it's like the house itself – the floor, the walls, the roof, and all the air and electricity trapped in between is dead quiet and sad too because Alec's not here.

It's an icy feeling, like musty smells and ghosts that each night now I lock out in the hallway. And I keep seeing Jackie's room as the quietest and coldest part of the house. I don't want to, but I imagine her lying in bed with her arms wrapped tightly around herself and her teeth chattering but no sound coming from them. I wish she would snore or talk in her sleep, then maybe I could go to sleep too; but somehow it's like her room is a million miles away and drifting further all the time.

Sleep should be a good friend; but it isn't. When you need it as a friend, it's never around. Funny, but there's something good about having Andy in the same room; it's a safe feeling. Jackie should bring her bed in here too. She climbed into bed with Andy on Friday night, but I think she figured she couldn't always be doing it.

Wednesday September 23rd

"For Christ sake, will you stop moping around as if you've lost your super-hero," Jackie yelled irritably at me after school. Then she cooled down, and must have regretted it because she shook her head at herself. "Look Mark, go out and do something with Andy, okay? Stick close to him. Think about him a little too, heh?"

How come she was calling me selfish? I've been helping her as much as I could. What was bloody expected of me? So I fished him out of the bedroom where he was staring at some Maths he couldn't do, and challenged him to a Test match in the sideway. We stuck a rubbish-bin against the garage doors, and I let him bat first. At first I thought it was going okay, especially when I let him hit the ball past me out onto the road. But when I returned from chasing it, he had gone. I found him in the garage digging one of Alec's best screwdrivers into the bench.

"Do you hate him?" he said to me, keeping his back to me and wiping his nose.

"A bit."

"How come he's allowed to go away?" he asked.

I thought of the conversation about Charlie going to the film when I wanted him to go roller-skating.

"Because he reckons we don't own each other," I said.

He didn't say anything for a minute.

"You know I was only joking when I told you about him having a girlfriend," he said slowly.

"Yeah, and I didn't believe you anyway," I answered.

"Do you reckon he's with that bitch now?" he asked, digging at the wood of the bench.

"He'll come back," I said. "He's our dad."

"Mum'll make him," Andy said, and now I could hear him crying. "I won't annoy him or anything. I'll do a lot of things to help him. I'll fix up his vegetables."

Friday September 25th

They say bad things come all together, and they're right.

122

Uncle Liam died early this morning. The lady next door came and told Jackie while we were having breakfast. It was all too much. Alec's going to be real hurt when he finds out. I hope I don't see Mrs McNamara around for a while either. Jackie's going to visit her later this afternoon.

Saturday September 26th

It's Grand Final day for the footy. I suppose I'll have to watch it on the TV. I sort of feel I should hang around on the weekends in case Jackie wants something. But the more I think about the footy and finals, the more I think about the one we went to two years ago.

It's a good memory and it has no right to hurt or make me feel bitter. Alec got home on the Friday night and said he'd been given four tickets at school.

"So, who's coming?" he had said, holding them up.

I volunteered straight away. Jackie hates footy. Now I'll tell you something. Andy is a real amateur when it comes to footy. No matter how hard I've tried to teach him about it, he's got a real mental block. He still doesn't even know the places on the field. He doesn't even watch the replays.

"I will," Andy had said.

"Good," said Alec. "And I'll give Alfredo a ring."

So that morning we had met Alfredo at a pub close by the ground, and would you guess it, but he brought his son. I mean the kid was only three then, and it was going to be packed. And Andy had two jumpers on even though it was a warm September day and a stupid knitted cap that looked like a tea-cosy; and he was carrying a comic and a big bag of sandwiches and fruit.

"What sort of tickets are they?" Alfredo had asked, as we walked down to the ground. Alec gave him his. He looked closely at the ticket, and stopped walking. "But this is a junior ticket?"

"They all are," said Alec casual like. "But a ticket's a ticket."

How embarrassing, I thought. Alec just barged through first, and didn't give the guy a chance to stop him in the crowd, so we all did the same.

Then he said: "There's only one place to watch a final, and that's in the outer behind the goal with the other peasants."

And no kidding, we had seating tickets. What a joke. I don't know why, but most of the thousands in the outer stand around at the top of the stairs leading up to it, so that once you've climbed them you can't go any further. They reckon they were there first. Alec pushed straight into them and he was yelling out over their heads: "Hey Bill . . . Frank . . . where's our spot you buggers . . . I've got the grog . . . Hey, there you are . . . excuse me mate . . . Jesus it was crowded at the bar . . . excuse me mate . . ."

I tell you, once you get settled though, and you're looking out over the enormous green oval, surrounded by the colours in the crowd and bathed by sunlight, you can't help stopping and smiling to yourself. It makes you feel you're in heaven at last. I remember that we'd just got there, and Andy wanted to know if it was time for lunch. He opened his bag and pulled out a squashed peanut-butter and banana sandwich. Because it was getting so crowded the smell of the sandwich hit the air and stayed trapped between all of us because he was sort of down there a bit. He offered it around. Everyone refused except Nicky, Alfredo's son. I don't know how he got it down. Next came a cucumber and egg sandwich. I'm sure most of the crowd weren't watching the game. Then I couldn't believe it; he wanted a hot-dog.

They were all amateurs. None of them knew how to watch football properly. All afternoon, they were going up and down to the dunnies, or buying hot-dogs or beer, or Alec was barracking for different sides all day and yelling out dumb things because he said you don't normally get the chance; while Andy sat in the filth on the ground and tried to read his comic aloud to Nicky. And then ten minutes into the last quarter, when Collingwood was getting beaten, Alfredo thought it was time to try and commit suicide, because he took his camera out, and started taking close-ups of people looking ugly and disappointed and pissed and very unfriendly. I'll tell you, just as well Collingwood got up to go on and win easily. And would you believe it. There were Alfredo and Alec and Andy celebrating with the Collingwood supporters, even singing their club song.

And I was exhausted from worry, and my team had lost, but no, we had to drop into about three pubs on the way home and talk to guys with missing legs and ears and prison records and strange accents. So when we finally flopped home at about 9:00pm with legs like lead, and mouths dry from screaming and walking, what's the first thing Jackie said, finishing off all the Creme Caramel, my favourite dessert: "And did you men enjoy your tough little game?" She said it like we were all babies.

And would you believe it? No kidding. Both Alec and Andy nodded their heads at the same time as if they were little kids. And the way I feel right now, I'd give anything to go through it again just to be with Alec. He made it kind of daggy the whole day; and yet exciting, and when you're with him, you're always meeting strangers and doing and saying things you wouldn't normally. And it's hard to believe that's the same person we lived with after the accident, and who deserted us.

Tuesday September 29th

When Alec left, he took almost nothing with him. I suppose it's good in a way because a little bit of him is still living here. And I kind of think he'll be back as soon as he's had a rest and begins to miss us. At night it's the hardest because that's when we seem the loneliest without him, and it's funny because there's three of us and one of him. I look at his things a lot, and tonight found some photographs that I don't remember seeing. I took the packet out to Jackie to show her. We looked at some prints of the garden and Andy and the stray dog. She finally settled on one print, resting it in her lap and taking a long puff of her cigarette. It was one she took herself at his students' party we had here. In it Lesley Anherbrat is sitting on the arm of Alec's chair, looking at him and smiling as if she owned him. I guess I got pretty angry.

"It was that bitch's fault," I said. "We were all right until he started teaching her."

She looked at me surprised.

"Whatever do you mean, Mark?" she asked.

I didn't feel like being careful any more or worrying about hurting other people's feelings.

"Well he was messing with her, wasn't he?" I said. "Where did he get to the night before the accident?"

She looked uneasy.

"Oh no, he was worried about her, but I don't think he made love to her," she said. She stopped and looked at me as if she was working out in her brain whether she should say what she said next. "He would have told me. He always told me when he was unfaithful."

Unfaithful. Just like that, as if everyone does it. Alec and Jackie? My mum and dad?

"Whaddya mean?" I asked dumbly.

She just looked at me.

"Well why did you let him?" I said, angrily. "Didn't it worry you?"

"Of course," she said. "It still hurts."

To be honest, I didn't know what to say next. I felt like I was growing up too quick all of a sudden. Finally: "Well what about all that talk about the police and Lesley Anherbrat. What was that all about?"

"Some relative was taking advantage of her," Jackie answered. "Alec tried to help her, and eventually decided he needed to involve the police."

Boy, now I was the one who was totally confused, and yet feeling sort of relieved.

"Well, why didn't anyone say anything about this to me?"

She stared at me. "Possibly we did the wrong thing. But your father has been unhappy. He needed to be left alone."

And then suddenly, for the first time for ages, I felt a little happy; like I had a big weight off my mind. I could feel I hadn't lost my dad.

"Why did he go to Queensland, then?" I asked.

"I'm not sure," she said, shrugging her shoulders. Her eyes started to water a little. "When some people become unhappy, they feel they would be worse to live with if they stayed. They also feel they're running out of time."

"For what?"

"For trying to find happiness, I suppose," she said.

"He was happy here," I said.

She looked at me, and her lip started to quiver. "Sometimes he was very unhappy."

"Does that mean he didn't like us?"

She got up and walked to the windows, and stared out at the garden.

"You'll have to ask him that," she answered eventually.

Then I remembered something.

"Uncle Liam said he had a restless spirit."

"Perhaps he wasn't a stupid old drunk after all," she said.

Thursday October 1st

When I arrived home, there were two post-cards from Alec lying on the coffee-table in the sunroom. I couldn't help getting all excited as I picked them up and read them. They were both a real disappointment. He said he was okay and

127

hoped we were okay; that he had had a good trip up, and that it was hot. And that really was it, except for apologising twice for leaving without saying goodbye to Andy and me. There was nothing about when he was coming back. Jackie acted as if she hadn't even bothered reading them, and Andy just looked at the pictures on them of banana trees and people with parrots sitting on their heads. He could have at least said that he was missing us a lot, like we're missing him.

Wednesday October 7th

"What are you doing at Christmas?" I asked Charlie.

"Working in my uncle's delicatessen and then nothin'," he answered.

"Want to go hitchin'?" I said. "We could go all the way up the coast and the surf beaches to Queensland."

"And see your dad?" he asked.

"Yeah."

"Great," he said, looking excited. "And we could stay there and get some bikes and girls and live on the beach and smoke dope and start up a band."

"Great," I said, trying to hide my disappointment. I knew his dad wouldn't let him, and Jackie probably wouldn't let me either.

And after school, Charlie said this real strange thing.

"You know, I reckon Billy was a deadshit," he said. "But we didn't do anythin' to help him; you know, back him against Whiles that day."

How come people are always expecting you to do things, like you've got a whole lot of power or something? What was I supposed to do? Punch up Whiles, or report him? I mean I told both Paul Kelly and Alec and they didn't do anything. And who's helping me now?

"Billy would have done it for you," Charlie said. "I bet he ends up in jail."

"Dad's here . . . Dad's here," said Andy, bursting in the back door, his eyes real wide. "He's out the front."

Jackie stared at me, and then the front door bell went.

"You'd better answer it," she said to Andy.

He came back, and Alec and him had their arms around each other. No kidding, I felt shy and like I was going to cry. His face was all brown, and he had his hair cut short, and there was a gold ear-ring in one of his ears. Jackie and him just stared at each other, and then they were hugging and not saying anything at the same time.

"How's things, Mark?" he asked over her shoulder.

"Good," I said dumbly.

"That's good," he said dumbly too, and came and held my hand, like it was a long handshake.

Boy, there were a lot of questions over tea. Everyone was talking excitedly and eating a lot, except Alec who seemed a bit embarrassed, like he was some sort of guest. And we all drank wine, and Andy asked about the parrots on people's heads, and no kidding before we knew it, it was ten o'clock. Alec then said he had forgot, and pulled out a gift each for all of us from his bag, and there was a lot of laughing about that too.

"Anyway, I must push off now," he said, standing up.

My throat went dry. I'm sure my mouth dropped like Andy's. Wasn't he home? Where was he going? I watched him get up, and suddenly I couldn't take it any longer.

"Whaddya think you're doing?" I said aggressively.

"Easy," he said, smiling at me.

"Whaddya doing? You've got to live with us," I said feeling my whole body vibrating. "What's going to happen to us?" He came towards me, but I got up and went around the other side of the table.

"It'll work out," he said, and I could see him shaking too. Jackie just sat there. No one was helping.

"Well, why d'ya come around acting like some sort of visitor?" I said.

"Let me explain . . ." he answered flashing looks at Jackie, "I've no right to pretend I can just come and go now . . ." But I didn't let him finish.

"Whaddya mean pretend? You're supposed to live here with us. You're my dad," and I pointed at Andy who was pale with fright. "And his."

He passed another look at Jackie; but this time she looked coldly back at him. He looked trapped.

"We can't talk about it like this," he said.

"We can never talk about anything," I yelled.

He started to leave.

"Mark, use your diary. Write it all down. You'll feel –"

"Get stuffed," I screamed at him, and came here into my room, and didn't watch him go. No kidding, I wouldn't let anyone in, and I just sat here for about an hour, and then started writing. I suppose Andy is sleeping with Jackie. It was bad before. Now it's like torture. What did we ever do to him?

Sunday October 25th

When I think about the argument with Alec last Sunday, I reckon I didn't give him much of a chance to talk. I guess I was very disappointed; didn't see the way things were. I don't think he'll ever come back if I treat him like that. He rang up during the week and spoke to Jackie, and came around today to take Andy to the zoo.

I answered the door. He stood there with his camera in his hand, and waited as if I wasn't going to ask him to come in. Jackie was out at her mother's, and it was crazy. We sat waiting in the sunroom and hardly said anything. I guess I was waiting for him to ask me along too, but he didn't.

I saw them pull up at about five, through the front-room

window. They sat talking in the car for a while, and then Alec drove off. Andy just stood there and watched him go.

"What did he say to you?" I said to Andy as soon as he came around the back.

"He said I could go and stay with him if I wanted to," he mumbled.

Wednesday November 4th

Word's finally getting around. I even told Charlie and Paul Kelly the truth. Jackie's friends and some relatives have begun to drop in for visits or ring up. Usually they don't mention anything at all and hope that Jackie will bring it up. But some have come right out with it and act real sure of themselves as if they are going to take over for a while and they spend their time telling Jackie that either he will be back soon or that she has the perfect chance to take another look at her life and ambitions. A friend of Alec's even dropped in and told her that she was better off because Alec was too suffocating. Jackie always looks as if she doesn't care and lets them go on planning her tactics for her in some war they see is happening.

Normally she hardly ever answers the phone any more, and she tells Andy and me to say she is out to some people. It's funny but sometimes we can start to laugh again and have a good time, then bang, she's worse than ever. Alec came on Sunday for a while and at one stage they were hugging, but when he left she was hopeless. Andy goes around with this long guilty look on his face like it's the end of the world. I've told him Alec will be back soon, and I know he will. And that's why when people drop in and start treating us like we're all sick or something, I feel real angry because they should realise also that there's nothing to worry about.

131

Sunday November 8th

Alec's become like one of those Sunday fathers. He said something today I didn't like the sound of.

"Sometimes it isn't until you're left alone that you find out how to do things," he said quietly, just to me. "My father never encouraged me to try things, and my mother always did things for me. And when I was at school, they told me what I should be doing and how to do it. Since I've been living alone, I've begun learning things for myself. I still want to learn. You ask me how you will get on without me. You'll learn the same way; without me always showing you."

"You can learn here," I said. "We won't pester you."

Friday November 13th

Jackie went out with this guy David for dinner. She's known him for years, and done some design work for this little shop he owns. He drives a new Datsun and knows all these big words when he talks. They got back early, and he came in for coffee, and we all talked about Alec for a while, and then he left.

"Look, your mother is smiling for a change," she said. I reckon she had drunk a lot of wine.

I know it's good that she went out to dinner, and that it made her happy, but it doesn't help get Dad back, does it?

Saturday December 5th

Summer has started, and the garden is overgrown from spring. The grass is too long, the vegetable patch is a mass of couch grass and weeds and twisted stems of the remains of vegetables of last season. No one sees it as important any more, and to be honest it's just too much work for us. I suppose really what should happen is Andy and me get together and have a go at it. It could make Jackie feel a bit better; a bit more optimistic. But I just can't bring myself to it, and Andy and me never really have worked as a team. And in a way I feel it was more Alec's garden than anyone else's, which kind of makes me feel angry because of the work the rest of us put into it. It makes us out to be sort of weak now, or the feeling we can't go places with Alec, or that we don't care about having fresh vegetables. We got some more chooks but Andy doesn't show the same interest in these ones. It's always left up to Jackie and me to take it in turns to clean their pen and make sure they get fresh water. It just all shouldn't be that way. But when I look out into the garden from the sunroom, I see Alec's body shining in the sun amongst the plants, and it gives me the creeps, because I can't help it, I just feel sad, and the last thing I want to do is rush out and start turning the soil over.

Saturday January 16th 1982

We've just got back from Apollo Bay. Jackie rented a house there for two weeks; it was all she could afford. Andy and me met some kids with surf-boards, and I reckon I learnt a little bit how to surf. Charlie was allowed to come down for a week too, and he met this great girl who was older than him. No kidding, everywhere we went Andy followed.

I remember on about the third night, Andy and me had gone down to the beach after tea. When we got back, Jackie was sitting in the half dark with a glass of beer and a cigarette. I really felt sorry for her, like she was waiting for something to happen, and didn't want to be on the holiday anyway.

Anyway a couple of days later she said to us: "Would you guys object to me inviting a friend down?"

And next moment she was on the phone, and on the following Saturday morning, a new Datsun rolled up.

Sunday January 17th

If someone asked me how come I couldn't tell my parents were going to break up, I'd probably say because they seemed so happy. I guess now that's how I saw them because that's the way I hoped they were. I mean I know they argued and he'd changed all of a sudden, but he wasn't coming home drunk and bashing Jackie or anything like the way the kids at school talk about their parents. Funny thing about that is that sometimes those families stick together – like they'd starve if they didn't.

But when I think about it, Alec is like two different guys; one who's a dad, and one who is all alone. And also when I think about it, it's like he tries to be busy and happy all the time otherwise he'd end up feeling like he was alone. I guess maybe he wanted someone to ask him if he was really happy. He's always acted too powerful to talk about it himself.

Maybe I should have tried harder to talk to him, but then why should it have been me? I'm still really just a kid. That's fair enough isn't it? I don't see why I should blame myself for not asking him. Let's face it, you'd reckon he had it made. He had a car; a good-looking wife to have sex with; a family that loved him; and a job that he got all excited about. So I don't see how I should have talked to him. That was Jackie's job. You'd reckon everyone's going around the world throwing their marriages away – and kids. And why go and fix up a home if you're not going to stick around and enjoy it? I might have been able to work a bit harder, but they were always his ideas. I reckon I can't be blamed for too much. I mean what would the perfect sort of son have done? I love him, don't I, and want him to come home. Jesus, what else does he want? It's like there's got to be a new adventure in his life all the time.

Jackie seems to want to talk about what's going to happen
to us. She reckons we should be able to keep the house while
she keeps up her two jobs. I know that Alec gives her some
money. She reckons Andy and me have to do more things
around the house, and that we should always see Alec as our
father, but one who lives somewhere else. She says Alec
can't just come back when he wants to now, and he's got to
show us that he's serious if he decides to. Andy never says
anything. He just drops his head when we talk serious. I
keep saying he should be allowed to come back when he
wants, and the sooner the better.

She seemed real excited when she got up this morning,
like she was going to have pups.

"Feel like some hard work?" she asked.

"What?" I said dopily.

"No questions," she said, putting her long hair into an
elastic band. "Go and get Andy, and then the both of you
fetch the sledge-hammer, crow-bar, and a spade and shovel
from the garage."

I don't know why, but I actually hurried into the house
to get Andy as if there was some kind of emergency. He
followed me out to the garage, then we joined Jackie who
was waiting under the Cypress.

"Hit there," she said, pointing at the concrete at the base
of the tree.

I raised the sledge-hammer and let it fall tentatively to the
ground we were standing on.

"Harder," she said.

"Give me a go," Andy said wrestling the sledge-hammer
off me. It was a struggle for him to raise it above his head,
but he brought it down with all the strength he had. But he

135

didn't stop there. He raised it about six times and crashed with accuracy on the same target each time. At first there were only chips and sparks, but then a crumbling followed. And he wouldn't let either of us take it off him. A final hit from him sent a crack of about twenty centimetres across the concrete. That's all we needed. The work took over two hours and when we had finished my back ached and palms were raw. And we were all soaked in sweat. I picked up my tee-shirt from the ground and wiped the salt out of my eyes. We had cleared and removed all the concrete in a radius of about two metres all around the base of the Cypress. The top-soil of earth which was like stone had also been turned and the hose lay on its side drenching the area. For a moment we all just heaved from tiredness.

"That makes me feel real satisfied," said Jackie, smiling in a way that it was impossible not to join in. "Let's see if we can get some new growth."

And she picked up the hose, and hit Andy right in the face with a jet of water.

EPILOGUE

It was Jackie who told me you could add a little bit to the end of a book. I'm in a position to say a few more things, since my last entry in my diary was three months ago. Alec hasn't dropped in for over a month, I reckon it is. I'm sure Jackie and him haven't been out for dinner or anything in that time because she would have told us. He's living in a flat in Carlton and believe it or not still works in the same restaurant. Jackie's been seeing David quite a lot. He's okay I suppose. Acts too smooth, I reckon, and he's over forty.

I've visited Alec about three times in his flat. It's small and of course there's no room for any garden. Each time he answers the door he looks rapt and hugs me, and we go in and he makes a cup of tea, and we sit and talk. Once we went out to a film together afterwards. I asked him last time I was there was he thinking of coming home. His face screwed up and he looked around him.

"I am home," he said.

Some more titles in Lions Teen Tracks:

☐ **Catch You On the Flipside** *Pete Johnson* £1.95
☐ **The Chocolate War** *Robert Cormier* £2.25
☐ **Rumble Fish** *S E Hinton* £1.95
☐ **Tex** *S E Hinton* £1.95
☐ **Breaking Up** *Frank Willmott* £1.95

All these books are available at your local bookshop or newsagent, or to order direct from the publishers, just tick the titles you want and fill in the form below.

NAME (Block letters) _____

ADDRESS _____

_____

Send to: Collins Childrens Cash Sales, PO Box 11, Falmouth, Cornwall, TR10 9EP

I enclose a cheque or postal order or debit my Visa/Mastercard to the value of the cover price plus:

UK: 60p for the first book, 25p for the second book, plus 15p per copy for each additional book ordered to a maximum charge of £1.90.

BFPO: 60p for the first book, 25p for the second book plus 15p per copy for the next 7 books, thereafter 9p per book

Overseas and Eire: £1.25 for the first book, 75p for the second book, thereafter 28p per book.

Credit card no: _____

Expiry Date: _____

Signature: _____

Some more titles in Lions Teen Tracks:

☐ **Tell Me If the Lovers are Losers** *Cynthia Voigt* £2.25
☐ **In Summer Light** *Zibby Oneal* £1.95
☐ **Happy Endings** *Adèle Geras* £2.25
☐ **Strictly for Laughs** *Ellen Conford* £1.95
☐ **The Warriors of Taan** *Louise Lawrence* £2.25
☐ **Second Star to the Right** *Deborah Hautzig* £1.95

All these books are available at your local bookshop or newsagent, or to order direct from the publishers, just tick the titles you want and fill in the form below.

NAME (Block letters) _____

ADDRESS _____

_____

Send to: Collins Childrens Cash Sales, PO Box 11, Falmouth, Cornwall, TR10 9EP

I enclose a cheque or postal order or debit my Visa/Mastercard to the value of the cover price plus:

UK: 60p for the first book, 25p for the second book, plus 15p per copy for each additional book ordered to a maximum charge of £1.90.

BFPO: 60p for the first book, 25p for the second book plus 15p per copy for the next 7 books, thereafter 9p per book

Overseas and Eire: £1.25 for the first book, 75p for the second book, thereafter 28p per book.

Credit card no: _____

Expiry Date: _____

Signature: _____

Lions reserve the right to show new retail prices on covers which may differ from those previously advertised in the text or elsewhere.

Some more titles in Lions Teen Tracks:

- ☐ **Come a Stranger** *Cynthia Voigt* £2.25
- ☐ **Waiting for the Sky to Fall** *Jacqueline Wilson* £1.95
- ☐ **A Formal Feeling** *Zibby Oneal* £1.95
- ☐ **If This is Love, I'll Take Spaghetti** *Ellen Conford* £1.95
- ☐ **Moonwind** *Louise Lawrence* £1.95

All these books are available at your local bookshop or newsagent, or to order direct from the publishers, just tick the titles you want and fill in the form below.

NAME (Block letters) _____

ADDRESS _____

_____

Send to: Collins Childrens Cash Sales, PO Box 11, Falmouth, Cornwall, TR10 9EP

I enclose a cheque or postal order or debit my Visa/Mastercard to the value of the cover price plus:

UK: 60p for the first book, 25p for the second book, plus 15p per copy for each additional book ordered to a maximum charge of £1.90.

BFPO: 60p for the first book, 25p for the second book plus 15p per copy for the next 7 books, thereafter 9p per book

Overseas and Eire: £1.25 for the first book, 75p for the second book, thereafter 28p per book.

Credit card no: _____

Expiry Date: _____

Signature: _____

Lions reserve the right to show new retail prices on covers which may differ from those previously advertised in the text or elsewhere.

Some more titles in Lions Teen Tracks:

☐ **Slambash Wangs of a Compo Gormer**
   Robert Leeson £2.50
☐ **The Bumblebee Flies Anyway** *Robert Cormier* £1.95
☐ **After the First Death** *Robert Cormier* £2.25
☐ **That Was Then, This Is Now** *S E Hinton* £1.95
☐ **Centre Line** *Joyce Sweeney* £2.25

All these books are available at your local bookshop or newsagent, or to order direct from the publishers, just tick the titles you want and fill in the form below.

NAME (Block letters) _____

ADDRESS _____

_____

Send to: Collins Childrens Cash Sales, PO Box 11, Falmouth, Cornwall, TR10 9EP

I enclose a cheque or postal order or debit my Visa/Mastercard to the value of the cover price plus:

UK: 60p for the first book, 25p for the second book, plus 15p per copy for each additional book ordered to a maximum charge of £1.90.

BFPO: 60p for the first book, 25p for the second book plus 15p per copy for the next 7 books, thereafter 9p per book

Overseas and Eire: £1.25 for the first book, 75p for the second book, thereafter 28p per book.

Credit card no: _____

Expiry Date: _____

Signature: _____

Lions reserve the right to show new retail prices on covers which may differ from those previously advertised in the text or elsewhere.